# RESTORING
## *justice*

A DARK ROMANCE DETECTIVE NOVELLA

ESME LENNON

# SIN

# CITY

Book cover by Marika Veil Covers

Edited by Ria at Moon and Bloom Editing

ISBN: 9781068528347

First edition 2025

# Please note:

The Tainted Town series and The Sin City series are intended to be a story-with-plot within a shorter book. These novellas are fast-paced and don't have as much depth as a full length novel. This is because my novella series are written with the purpose of giving slower readers a story line to follow, plot, and spice, but with a short page count. Please keep this in mind while reading.

# Trigger
## warnings

This book is intended for adult readers only, due to the content included.

Trigger warnings:

Mention of sexual assault, kidnapping, explicit sex scenes, 10 year age gap, violence, talks of drugs and alcohol, use of a gun, blood/description of injury, drink spiking, stalking, anxiety, vomiting, restraints.

To the eldest daughters.
You'll always be a warrior in my eyes.
Know your worth.

# *Playlist*

1. Hailee Steinfield – Dangerous

2. Bad Omans – THE DEATH OF PEACE AND MIND

3. X V I & Nocturn – Dirty Little Secret

4. The Weeknd – Die For You

5. Unions – Sex and Candy

6. Maroon 5 – Animals

7. Beyoncé – Crazy in Love

8. Paolo Nutini – Iron Sky

9. Ariana Grande – Into You

10. Lena Fayre – This World

11. RAIGN – Don't Let Me Go

12. The Weeknd – In Your Eyes

"Nothing inspires forgiveness quite like revenge."

– Scott Adams

# Contents

# RESTORING
## justice

I need to stay professional...
but she's too tempting to ignore.

# 1

## SASKIA

"As long as his football team isn't in his bio, then you're good." My eyes dart to my phone, pulling up the *At a Bar* dating app to check my date's profile, looking for anything that indicates he's a football lover. And just when I thought I was free, I see *Philadelphia Eagles* staring back at me.

I gulp as I gaze at my own reflection in my dressing room mirror, my hair in rollers and my body wrapped in a silk robe. I ignore the twisting feeling in my stomach as a familiar sense of dread weighs on my shoulders.

*I can do this.*

I can't back out of another date, so I shake my head at my FaceTime call, hoping that my best friend, Indie, is reassured. She's always been a good read of character, so I usually trust her judgement, but I've cancelled twice with Chris already. I've seen no red flags and he seems great, so far.

I loved dating when I was twenty-one. I was fresh on the scene and enjoying life, experiencing the many types of men and what I should expect from one in the long term. It showed me how disappointing they can be, which is why I focused more on my job than dating as I entered my mid twenties.

"Go for a red lip! Black hair and a red lip is the perfect combo." Indie shouts down the phone, my eyes hovering over my selection of lipsticks. Spotting a cherry red one, I pick it up and apply it onto my lips, rubbing them together a few times so it's spread evenly. Rifling through my dressing table, I shove my makeup to one side and begin taking out my curlers. A little bounce for my medium length hair, but a little extra length compared to my usual naturally tight waves.

"Outfit?" I hold up a black teacup dress with long sleeves and a flared leg and a black playsuit. Placing the first in front of me, I hold it up to Indie on the phone, and then swap with the other while she makes humming noises.

"The dress." She nods with certainty. "Your legs are made for that dress." My eyes glance down at both outfits before I hang the playsuit back up on the clothing rack. Slipping out of my robe, I sling it onto my stool and step into the dress, my eyes glancing to my phone to make sure Indie isn't anywhere public. We've been best friends since we were born, so seeing me half naked isn't a shock to her. She's used to it by now.

Chucking on some open toe heels and smoothing the front of my dress down, I twist my body to check the back. "Damn." I surprise myself when I put in a little effort.

"Damn, indeed, Sas. Now get your ass in a cab before you're late."

Her hang up is instant as I hear the two little beeps of the call ending. I'm not shocked at her sudden departure; we don't do goodbyes. Hang ups mean we talk again later, which means Indie will be expecting an eleven o'clock phone call after my date.

The date I am no longer interested in attending, but being a chronic people pleaser means I put everyone's feelings above my own. So, I pull up the cab booking app and book the quickest cab and make my way downstairs.

My home is small, but it's perfect for me. With no pets and no partner, I have this three bedroom town house all to myself. A red and white theme throughout, my favorite color combination gives the house brightness with character. Retro wall prints, heart patterned pillows, and a room filled with my clothes and makeup; it's exactly how I want my own home. A few streets away from Casamount's Courthouse, I live within walking distance from my job and rarely have to use my car. Old neighbors either side so no complaints, a decent sized back garden for when I want to work out in the sun, and a convenience store right around the corner. This is where I feel at home.

Loud buzzing pulls me from my internal thoughts as I make it out my front door, trying to read the text I received and locking the front door at once. I see the cab notification and glance over my shoulder, seeing the yellow car pull up outside my steps. I try to fight against my stiff lock, whispering curse words under my breath, until I hear the bolt twist. Yanking my keys from the door, I shove them into my black purse and hop into the cab without successfully twisting an ankle. Fighting the anxiety clawing inside my stomach, I try to ignore my thumping heart and dry throat as my nerves threaten to get the better of me.

*Deep breaths.*

I'm not cancelling. I'm not letting my mind convince me this is a mistake when I'm my own worst enemy. I'm taking control and I'm letting myself have a good time tonight.

The Rose Tavern comes into view, the pink strobe lights outside illuminating the wooden carved sign, as a queue of people chatter outside. Pulling up at my destination, I thank the cab driver and give him a ten-dollar tip, before shuffling my way out the door and towards the building.

Glancing down at my phone, I take another look at Chris's At a Bar photo and take in his mousy hair, blue eyes and dimples, before glancing at the clock. It's exactly seven o'clock, so I'm right on time. Ignoring the queue for drop ins, I head straight over to the petite bald man on the door, and tell him the table confirmation number Chris sent me. He flicks through a tablet, my eyes gazing over his stubble and he repeats the number eighteen over and over again.

"Ah! Found you!" He gasps, his sudden enthusiasm startling me. "Your date is already here." He enters through the door, holding it open for me as he gestures with his hand for me to follow him.

It's dark and chilly inside, the walls designed to look exactly like caves as water trickles down them on a constant loop. Dull pink lighting illuminates the room just enough for it to be safe to move around, with a small candle on each table for a little extra lighting. The scent of alcohol mixing with vanilla candles almost makes me nauseous, and I silently pray the smell won't be there when I eat my food. There's quiet jazz music playing from speakers around the room, as the full tables of people indulge in their own conversations.

A table in the far right corner comes into sight with a seated male sipping on a glass of wine. I squint, trying to make out his appearance, but he doesn't look familiar, so my eyes dart elsewhere. It's not until we are close enough to the man that I notice the number eighteen on the table, my body nearly retracts as Chris's image flashes in my mind. The man at the table is at least twenty years older, with salt and pepper hair, obvious wrinkles and a five o'clock shadow. I try to ignore his reddened hands and large fingers as he sips wine, but my mind then focuses on his stained teeth.

Oh lord. I've been catfished.

By a fifty year old man.

I want to scream at him; cause a scene for the time he's wasted. I spent hours on hair and makeup, finding the right outfit and being on time, just to be faced by a man who could be my father.

But my empathy gets the better of me. I know what I *should* do, but I can't bring myself to actually leave him here. I feel compelled by my own kindness to sit down and have a drink with him. He lied and used my trust against me, yet I'm the one who feels horrible for backing out.

I groan. One goddamn drink and then I'm out of here.

"Your table." The waiter puts his hand out to the empty chair opposite Chris and quickly makes a dash for it, as Chris stands to his feet.

"Saskia!" He grunts as he gets up, his arms open wide as he pulls me in for an embrace. My body is pulled against his, his sweaty scent mixed with tobacco. "So lovely to meet you!" He pulls away, his hands on my shoulders as he gives me a once over.

Whatever photoshop magic he used on his At a Bar photos, he could win awards for.

"You, too." I nod, wiggling my way out of his grip and sitting in my chair before he can pull it out for me. "You look different from your photos!" I try to joke, but I hear the nervous laughter in my voice. He pours me a glass of white wine that was already on the table as I tuck myself in, trying to look anywhere other than at this man.

"Ahh!" He chuckles, sliding over my full glass. "I had them cleaned up. They're photos of me from twenty years ago!" He gulps his wine, nearly finishing a full glass faster than he poured it. "I was a looker, wasn't I?" Winking, he raises his eyebrows at me as he laughs low and husky.

I nearly choke on my wine.

"Yeah! Yeah, you were." I nod, my brain internally figuring out whether to laugh or cry. I settle on a large sip of wine.

The quicker I finish, the quicker I can leave. I debate on bringing up the cab app to book one in, but I'm distracted by Chris's sudden voice. "What do you do for work, sweetheart?" He leans forward, and I don't miss the way his eyes drink in my cleavage.

Ew, patronising.

"I'm a reporter." I nod, taking another large sip. I don't feel comfortable telling him my actual job title, so I settle for an envelope term. "How about you?"

"I'm a cop." He lets the word roll off his tongue as he leans forward, his eyes once again dropping to my chest. "I'll soon be a deputy with a promotion heading my way."

My body's instant reaction is to recoil. I see the police every day at my job. Being a court reporter means the many times police are a testifying witness in court, I'll see them on the stand. But I have never seen this man in my life. Never at the courthouse and never at the station.

Alarm bells immediately ring in my mind, my nerve endings suddenly buzzing with adrenaline. I can't think straight as danger clouds my ability to be calm and collected. I'm never going to get out of a situation by panicking, but I can't stop my body from reacting this way.

"Congratulations." I force through my labored breaths, trying to seem engaged in our conversation still. "I'm just going to the bathroom quickly." I smile, trying to pick my purse up from the floor, but as I look down, I have double vision. Everything is blurred and moving in circles, my eyes heavy and slow.

Now, my body is on delay. I can't navigate my thoughts around this fog clouding my mind. Sound is distorted and echoing around me. Suddenly, I feel like I have weights on my shoulders and my legs can't handle it.

What is happening? One glass of wine doesn't do this to me.

Realization smacks me in the face.

I've been drugged and I'm losing consciousness.

I should do something, anything, to help myself, but my mind communicating to my body is hitting a language barrier. Nothing is getting through.

And just as it dawns on me how much danger I'm in, everything around me begins fading, and suddenly everything is black.

I should have trusted my gut.

# 2

# MITCHELL

The migraine threatening to appear behind my right eye is the result of another sleepless night. With multiple open cases and an empty apartment, my time is better spent digging into case files with a fresh pair of eyes. Being a police detective means I feel guilty for being off the job. If revisiting an old case can solve one, then I see no issue with what I'm doing.

Except, I haven't slept in twenty-four hours. And I'm preparing for a twelve-hour shift.

I need fresh coffee and a cold shower.

"Did you even do what I asked you to do?" Jules, my partner, gives me her best unimpressed look with her arms across her chest and her eyebrows raised. Her long black hair is tight in a ponytail and her slim figure is dressed in all black workwear. She attaches her gun to her holster and clips her badge and ID to her pants waistband.

I pinch the bridge of my nose as I inhale a deep breath. "No, Jules." I groan, walking away from her and towards the break room to get some fresh coffee. "I'm not taking selfies just for you to make me a dating profile. I'm thirty-five, not dead."

A chuckle escapes her lips as she pours us both a cup of coffee in disposable cups. "You're a workaholic who doesn't know how to flirt. You need help." She states plainly, heading towards our desks in the main room.

"I don't need help." I grunt, wiggling my mouse at my desk and loading up my emails.

I haven't dated anyone serious in over ten years and I haven't met someone I'm remotely interested in.

*Well, maybe one person.*

I definitely need help, but I'm not telling Jules that. She'd team up with her wife to find me a girlfriend and I'd rather chew on razor blades than go through that.

"Meeting in my office, all of you." Captain Wallace demands as he opens his office door. Jules and I follow behind Detective

Hackett and Detective Marten, entering Captain Wallace's office where Sergeant Fields is already waiting.

"We were just notified that a waiter called in a suspicious man carrying out a young woman from The Rose Tavern a couple hours ago. She had one drink and passed out." Captain Wallace takes a moment to load something up on his computer.

"Any leads?" I question. We've been on a very distant trail with this rapist. He's smart and tactical. He knows how to keep himself sheltered.

"Here." Turning the computer around, traffic camera footage of a large male carrying a young woman over his shoulder. She's floppy and unresponsive, unaware of the danger she's getting into.

"Has anyone been reported missing matching her description?" Jules asks, jotting down notes in her notepad.

"None yet, but we have the phones manned in case a call comes in." Sergeant Fields answers.

"Do we know which way he headed?" The words leave my mouth as my gaze is fixed on the pixelated screen. It's paused on the rapist and the victim, and I try to memorize as much as I can. Her black dress, her black hair, his large build, the faint bald spot on his crown.

"According to traffic cam footage he's on York Street. His vehicle was last seen between Baker and York street.

"Isn't that one massive storage unit?" Fields asks.

"Yeah, Better Storage, been there for decades. He's been untraceable up until now, but this might be our first chance to save one of his victims. Now, without knowing which unit he's using, it will take hours to search that place top to bottom, so I called in a favor with the K-9 unit. They're going to meet you there and let the dogs help. With what we know about this man, he likely hasn't done anything yet. He likes to wait at least twelve-hours to make sure they're weak. Proceed with caution and watch each other's six. Go, do your thing, but be careful. We need this arrest to stick."

Grabbing my gun from my pocket, I check my bullets before slotting the magazine back in. Giving Jules a nod, we leave the office and head towards our desks, grabbing our police jackets. Detectives Hackett and Marten do the same as we prepare for a raid.

We may be a small team investigating crimes within Casamount, but we always have each other's backs. No one goes alone. This team is like my family, and I'll make damn sure every single member is safe before I am.

🍒 · 🍒 · 🍒 · 🍒

A building of storage rooms; the perfect place to take a victim. No one stays around long enough for sound complaints, it's not a popular location and people don't ask questions.

I don't want to believe it's this easy. Rapists have never made our job easy before, and something tells me it won't be easy this time.

The K-9 unit ran through here like a storm. The sniffer dogs alerted by one unit - 2B. I'm just glad the cadaver dogs didn't find anything.

Me and Jules take the front with Casamount officers watching our backs. Each step we take sounds painfully loud in this silent building. No people, no background noise - nothing. Just a possible kidnap victim and our chance of catching a rapist.

The red and tall door stares me down and the metallic '2B' sign looks back at me, my ear instantly pushing up against the door. I hear no sounds or anything out of the ordinary which only raises my guard higher. This place is eerie and strange; it feels like the kind of place where secrets are kept alive.

Holding up three fingers, I count down before Jules carefully unlocks the unit. The manager didn't want to help but court order trumps bad decisions. As the mechanical door rolls up, I can't help but wince at the sound. No quiet breach for us then. Keeping my gun raised, I flick a light switch and instantly gulp as my eyes take in what I'm looking at. The unit has been halved by a makeshift wall and door which is separating the back of the unit from the front. I ignore the empty moving boxes and old furniture and head towards the second door. It's shut, but there's no lock function. Signalling Jules, we breach through the door with guns raised, this time, this makeshift room has a pop up workshop. Everything a handyman needs; tools, nuts, bolts, screws. Why hide this back here? It's too perfect.

My eyes float around the room, my senses still on high alert, and I spot a large box in the back corner of the room. The sight instantly feels unnatural to me, the storage boxes are in the room before, not this one. I walk over, my hands gripping the box and moving it behind me.

*Another goddamn door. It must lead into the unit next door.*

I don't wait around for someone else.

My leg muscles contract as my foot makes contact with the wooden door, the wood splintering and falling as the door swings open. My gun raised, I sweep the room, but it's almost empty. No light or furniture in here except a metal bed frame with a mattress.

And a woman.

My eyes fall onto the female tied to the frame with rope, both her hands and feet bound. Her clothes are gone and her golden skin exposed, her underwear being the only clothing remaining. I can't see her face because her dark hair is covering it, and my stomach suddenly sinks. She's not moving and I can't see her chest rising and falling.

Panic takes over my body and kicks me into action. Pocketing my gun, I take a few steps to the bed and grasp her cheeks, pulling her face towards me.

My heart stops for a second.

Closed eyes, her mouth slightly agape, light bruises around her throat.

I know her.

Usually focused and formal, the complete opposite to her weak and fragile state.

"Jules!" I shout, my panic turning into anger. "Get that ambo in here!"

Holding my fingers to her neck, I feel for a pulse. A faint beating feels against my fingers and relief fills my body.

"Saskia?" I wobble her face, trying anything I possibly can to wake her up. Not knowing if it's the drugs or if she's been knocked out, my actions become erratic. "Saskia, come on, wake up." I say, lifting her eyelids for some sort of light reaction.

"Shit." I grunt. Pulling out a pocket knife from my jacket, I cut the ropes binding her to the bed, her body hopelessly flopping down on the dated mattress. I look for a blanket or anything I can wrap her in, but there's nothing in here except this bed.

I can't leave her undressed for gawking eyes, so I unzip my jacket and wrap it around her, lifting her body so I can slide in her arms and zip it up.

"Jules, how long does it take to come up the stairs?" I shout, my voice shaking as the anger drives me.

"They're here!" Jules runs into the room, two EMT's trailing her as they sling their bags down to help Saskia.

"Oh my god!" Jules gasps, her eyes glued onto Saskia's unconscious state. "Is that Saskia?" She recoils, her face scrunched.

I can't stop my heart from pounding in my chest. We are taught how to tone our feelings down for this job, yet sometimes they push through. Finding a victim is bad enough, but when it's someone you know, even if they are just someone you cross paths with at work, it makes you feel like dread is drowning you.

Pushing the nausea back down, I focus my attention back on the issue at hand. Someone did this to Saskia and they're still out there, possibly scouting for his next victim. She's safe, for now, and in the care of medical professionals, but the next ones might not be so lucky, so finding this sick rapist is our only option.

I need to follow our only lead.

"I'm riding with you." I announce to the EMT's, hopping in the back of the rig and sitting down next to the middle aged man working on Saskia. She has tubes in her arms already and oxygen hooked up to her nose. Still unconscious, but her stats are improving.

We got to her just in time. Any later and she might not have made it alive to greet her abductor.

"Detective Alvarez?" Her voice is quiet and hoarse, the words barely register in my brain.

My attention immediately darts towards Saskia, her eyes struggling to open as she blinks slowly. "Just hold on, Saskia. We'll be at the hospital in a minute." I want to grasp her hand for reassurance to show her it's okay and she's safe now, but I don't want to push her further into this nightmare she's living, so I settle for a smile.

But I don't know if she sees it. Her eyes can't stay open and her attempt to stay responsive is in vain.

Unconsciousness grabs her and pulls her back under.

# 3

## SASKIA

My brain is telling itself to shut off my pain receptors. It's trying to protect itself from the inevitable. Reliving what I just went through.

I have to give a statement, but the words burn holes in my throat. I wish it was as simple as telling someone what happened to me, but I've had to do so much already. My fingernails scraped, my rope burns and bruised throat photographed, a rape kit conducted. I don't remember anything happening to me and other than the restraints, my body isn't hurting, so I'm praying to whoever is above that nothing worse happened to me.

I deal with cases like these in court every single day, but being a victim shines a completely different light on what these people go through.

What *I* went through.

I'm giving up dating for the foreseeable future. Being single is better than meeting a date from hell.

"Hey." The low voice makes my body jump, my hands clinging onto the side of the hospital bed. I don't realize my eyes have been open and glued to the ceiling.

Focusing my eyes to where the sound came from, they fall onto Detective Alvarez sitting in the corner, a coffee in one hand and a paper in the other. "Detective Alvarez." I roll onto my left side so I can see him better. "You didn't have to stay." I smile, my eyes heavy. I take in his appearance as I try to tell my exhausted brain to focus. Dark, short hair, brown eyes, and his usual stoic expression. Definitely the same man I see in court every now and then.

"I wanted to." He nods, his smile not quite reaching his eyes. I wonder what's on his mind. There's something going on behind those eyes of his, but I don't want to push.

My lips open to respond but his ringtone stops the sound from escaping my mouth. I expect him to answer, considering his job, but I hear him push a button and the ringtone ends.

"Are you here for my statement?" I ask, bile threatening to make its way up my throat  at the thought of even explaining my date last night.

This time, his mouth opens to speak but he's interrupted by his ringtone again. He sighs, checking the screen but ending the call again with one click.

"You can answer it, Detective Alvarez." I say, guilt teasing its way to the surface as I keep him from his job.

He shakes his head. "It's not important." He reassures me, pressing some other buttons on his phone before sliding it into his pocket. "And you can call me Mitch. We've crossed paths enough times to be on a first name basis."

A light chuckle escapes my lips. "Please don't let me keep you from your work, Mitch. I'm fine, I promise." The lie burns my tongue as the words leave my mouth. Part of me wants him to stay so I'm not alone, but most of me is weighed down by embarrassment.

"You aren't keeping me from anything. I want to be here." The words are sincere and I have to fight tears from forming. The urge to cry is suddenly so powerful, but the feeling of sadness isn't forming my tears. I don't know what to feel right now; this experience is new to me. I feel violated and dirty and

I'm carrying so much disgust aimed at my body knowing *he* touched my bare skin.

"It's a little awkward," the words escape my lips before I can think it through. "Considering we know each other from court." I shrug. His eyes are focused on me, but he doesn't say anything. "But I suppose you don't go to court to make friends. You go to close cases." I've seen his whole team in court before, but I wouldn't consider a single one of them a friend. They're acquaintances who have the same legal views as I do. We fight on the same side, but it doesn't mean we are all bonded together.

"Hey." The softness in Mitch's voice pulls me from the daydream I didn't realize I was in. He stands beside me, somehow making it from the chair and across the room to next to my bedside, eyes flicking from my purple throat to my eyes. I don't miss his throat bobbing as he swallows, but words don't form.

My eyes burn as they have that urge to fill with tears again, but I fight against it. I'm not allowing myself to cry because of a sympathetic gaze. I don't want to be looked at like a victim, because then I have to admit that I am one.

And I'm not ready for that.

I can't stand being in this dull hospital room anymore. I need to be at home in the safety of my house. Forcing my torso upwards, I ignore the fatigue pulling me down and try to pull the cannula out of my arm.

"Sas, don't." Mitch's hands are suddenly on top of mine, blocking my vision and stopping my hand movements. "Let's get a nurse to do that. Then I can take you home."

The sudden skin contact makes me freeze my movements, and I almost recoil. I have to remind myself that it's Mitch's hands. I might not know him well, and I'm not exactly thrilled this is how we are formally introduced, but it's a slight comfort knowing it's his hands and not Chris's.

Nodding, I agree to stop removing the cannula and wait for a nurse. I don't remember much, but I remember my lack of clothes. I don't know what Chris did with them, or if that's even his real name. And then it hits me. "Do you know where my phone is?" I question Mitch as he enters the room with a nurse. I pat around the bed, search the bedside table and look for my bag of belongings, but I come up empty handed.

"No belongings were found at the scene and anything they did find has been taken into evidence. Is there an emergency?" Mitch asks, pulling his phone from his pocket and pressing some buttons.

I try to ignore the nurse removing the cannula as the adhesive holding it burns my skin as it's removed, and I hiss in response. Her apologies are instant. "Yes, there's an emergency." My hand wipes my stray hairs from my forehead. "I was supposed to ring Indie at eleven. God, I bet she's losing her mind." Still hunting for the phone I know isn't here, panic fires in my veins at the realization that Indie is probably panicking right now.

"Eleven in the morning?" Mitch's brows pull together as he looks at his watch. "You have three hours, yet."

*Oh my God.*

"Eleven last night!" I can barely keep myself from losing my mind. This is the last thing I need to happen right now. "She's going to call the cops. It's our rule." My head falls into my hands, knowing I'm now another burden to the police department. First kidnapped, now missing. They're going to think I'm the girl who cried wolf.

"Hey," Mitch's hands pull mine from my face, his face level with mine. "Calm down. I'll make a call and we'll get this straightened out. Write down Indie's number so I can contact her."

Mitch doesn't even give me a chance to thank him before he's walking around my hospital room and making calls.

Part of me wants to call Indie myself to let her know what has happened, but most of me is grateful Mitch is handling it.

She'll want details and I don't want to give them the time of day. Knowing her, she'll be purchasing a gun and finding Chris herself.

The nurse places a pile of sweats at the end of the bed and gets me to sign release forms. I stare at the sweats but I don't recognize them. I pull the black joggers and black hoodie open to inspect further, and I notice the mens clothing tag inside.

"That's all I had in my car." Mitch points towards the sweats I'm holding, his phone pulled away from his ear as he speaks quietly to me.

I nod, trying to keep my smile from turning into a full blown grin. "Thank you." I whisper, trying to not interrupt his phone conversation.

He turns around to face the door after seeing me rising to my feet. I'm assuming he's giving me some privacy, so I proceed with getting dressed. The sweats are a little big for me, but they're comfortable and they smell divine, so I don't complain. Sandalwood and mint invades my nostrils, the scent clinging to Mitch's sweats and making the universal hospital smell fade.

"All good." I say in Mitch's general direction, hoping he hears me to know the coast is clear and I'm fully clothed. I check for any belongings I might have, but the only thing I'm leaving behind is the hideous inpatient gown and a bowl of warm pineapple from the cafeteria.

"My partner, Jules, is trying to get hold of Indie now." Mitch reassures, holding his arm out and guiding me out towards the exits. His hand falls on my lower back, and while I know the contact should make me feel uncomfortable, I know he's doing it for reassurance. "She tried to file a missing persons report, but it hadn't been twenty-four hours, so she wasn't able to. The desk clerk said he nearly had to arrest her due to her aggressive nature."

Of course she nearly got arrested. "Sounds like Indie." I wince. "At least I know she'll fight for me." I breathe a laugh.

Exiting the hospital, Mitch opens the passenger side door to a navy Range Rover before shutting the door. He hops in, presses the ignition and begins driving.

Silence fills the car as the DAB radio takes its time connecting to the signal. I try to focus on objects outside, anything that catches my attention, but I'm hyper aware of the silence.

The sound of Mitch clearing his throat makes me jump from the sudden noise. "Just so you know, I'll fight for you, too." He says the statement so bluntly, like it's a normal thing to say to someone. "So will the rest of the team. I won't rest until he's brought to justice."

I don't miss the side glances Mitch keeps flicking my way and I'm suddenly conscious of every move I make. He's just declared his power of protection for me, but passes it off so casually. I suddenly feel like a schoolgirl again, sentences unable to be made because I'm too focused on my blushed cheeks.

*This is embarrassing.*

After five minutes, I think I've finally found the right response. My mouth opens to respond to Mitch, but he cuts me off.

"I'm here for you, Saskia. What you went through isn't easy. You're brave-"

"Please don't." The words choke me. I inhale a shaky breath. "I'm sorry. I just can't talk about it." I can't look at him, so I let my gaze wander off out the windshield. "If I start, I'll never stop crying."

"Okay." The words are barely a whisper from Mitch's lips. "This is your street, right?"

His change of subject makes me recoil and takes me a second to process it. My eyes focus on my white, two story home and relief floods my body.

This is normalcy.

"Mmhm." I nod, unbuckling my belt. "Thank you so much for staying with me."

Mitch just nods like it's not a big deal and hops out the car. My hands fall on the door handle, but Mitch is already opening it from the other side.

"You don't have to be a gentleman." I joke. "I know what you detectives are really like."

"And what's that?" He plays along, holding his hand out so I can make the small jump out of his car.

"Addicted to your phone, married to the job." I answer, Mitch handing me my new door keys.

He laughs, shrugging but not denying it. "Speaking of phones," he hands over a cheap black one. "Here's a burner until you can get a new one. Also I had your locks changed. We didn't recover your bag so I wanted to make sure you were safe in your own home."

I take the small phone and have a quick look. Nothing special but it'll get me by for now. "Thanks," I nod because words evade me right now. Stepping up to my front door, Mitch waits on the outside, grabbing something from his pocket.

He hands over a small piece of white card. "Call me if you need me. Anytime, okay?" He questions, his eyes stuck on mine as he waits for an answer.

I nod, taking the small piece of card and taking a quick peek. It has his number and name, along with his job title and email.

"Thank you," I pause. "For everything." It's not the thanks he deserves, but it's all I can pull together right now. I don't even want to know what would've happened if he didn't show.

With a brief nod, he's walking back to his car, his phone ringing in his pocket. I take a step back and begin shutting the door when Mitch shouts my name. "Eyes open." He instructs, his first and second fingers flicking in between his eyes and me.

I close the front door and fasten the locks, double checking they're secured. I make sure all windows are shut and the back door is locked before I retreat to the bathroom and turn on the shower. Steam fills the room as the reflection staring back at me begins to disappear. I see my face one minute and the next minute, I'm gone.

*Eyes open.*

The words replay in my head as I stand aimlessly under the boiling water. It feels like pin pricks assaulting my body as the water makes contact with my skin, but I don't want the pain to stop. I want to burn *his* touch from my body, erasing everything he did to me. I grab my loofah and scrub the sting from my assaulted skin. But I can't stop. I won't.

Not until I feel clean.

Sitting with my knees pulled close to my chest, I lose all track of time as my tears fall like a river. My emotions are numb, yet I can't control them.

I don't know how long I stay in the shower, long enough for the sting of the heat to turn to icy pin pricks. Long enough for my fingertips to wrinkle and my body feel dizzy. Long enough to know every place he touched me, marked me. I have red marks all over my skin. Anywhere he touched me is now raw. Damaged. Broken.

*Tainted.*

I lay in bed, staring aimlessly at my ceiling. I memorize each groove and curve, the textured pattern distracting my brain enough to go a minute without feeling dirty. I never noticed the design on the ceiling before. It's unique and dainty and adds character to my home.

Five minutes without thinking about it.

I sigh, waiting for the tiredness to hit my eyes. I want to sleep, to shut my mind off from letting it sink into that dark place. But I just can't. I'm exhausted, yet my mind won't shut off.

It's my own personal hell.

The deafening silence is interrupted by my burner phone ringing on my bedside table, my arm stretching out to reach it. I look at the number and recognize it instantly. I don't know how she got this number, and I don't know what she's been told, so I take a deep breath and prepare myself before answering.

"Hey, Indie."

# 4

# SASKIA

If eyes burned holes when they stared at someone, I'd be a damn good colander. I felt safe at work; I still feel safe, but now people notice me. Word travels fast around the courthouse, and whether it's to help a case or not, people love knowing all the juicy details.

Making the decision to return to work was easy. I want normality and to pretend like my *date* with Chris never happened, which means I'm returning to my workaholic schedule. If there's one place I'm safe, with cameras and law enforcement, it's the courthouse. Nothing will happen to me here.

I don't even know if Chris will return. From what Mitch has told me, Chris's M.O means he doesn't return to victims.

But I'm not one of his usual victims.

He wasn't finished with me. I don't want to play the game of how a sociopath thinks, but something in my gut tells me that he'll be back for me. He doesn't like loose ends. Certainly not the kind that can remember his face, that can give evidence against him. Despite being roofied and struggling to remember certain parts of the night, his face is imprinted on my brain. My face scrunches up as I fall deep into thought. Is he even called Chris? Now that I think about it, he doesn't look like a Chris.

The warm presence placed on my shoulder makes me flinch.

I turn instantly, my body triggering my survival instincts as my brain takes me back to a few nights ago. "Judge Donelly." My eyes skim over her black robe, short brown hair and blue eyes. "Sorry." I shrug, trying to find the right words to explain my edginess, but nothing forms.

"No, don't apologize." She waves me off, but her eyes are glued to me. I can already tell the pity party is about to show up, her brows pulled together and her eyes sunken. "I'm surprised you're back to work. Are you okay?"

I clear my throat and scan my eyes over the empty courtroom. I don't even know why I'm standing here. A moment of silence maybe? Shrugging my shoulders, I shake my head and force a smile. "I'm fine." The words are bitter on my tongue.

Judge Donelly's shoulders sink, and that's when I know she doesn't believe a word leaving my mouth. She can tell when someone's lying, I'll give her that.

"I don't want to talk about it." I say, swallowing back the wad of saliva in my throat. I'm hoping the smile on my face pushes her along, but she's still looking at me like a helpless kitten. "I just want to move on." My final attempt at getting the Judge to drop it, and my last attempt at a sentence before my eyes burn with tears.

"Okay." She nods. I attempt to walk away, but she grasps both my hands and pulls me to face her. I can see the determination swirling inside her eyes, and it makes me grateful for a second knowing I don't have to face her for a case. "Just promise me you'll give the police everything you can, so they can catch that son of a bitch."

I've never heard her cuss before, so the sudden use of that word makes a laugh escape my lips. I nod, reassuring her I'll give them all I have.

"And when his case is presented in front of this court," she leans closer and looks around us, making sure we are alone. Lowering her voice to a whisper, she looks me dead in the eye and says "we'll bury him."

I've seen all the tricks lawyers play to help their clients, but when a judge wants someone to go down, they're going down like a sunken ship.

"Sorry to interrupt." The words cut through the moment me and Judge Donelly were having so quickly, almost like we were conspiring to break some rules. Turning, I notice Mitch with his partner, Jules, waiting by the court door. "We need to talk about your statement." Mitch says, holding up a notepad as he softly smiles.

"Feel free to use my office." Judge Donelly calls out. "I'm off to the Enchantment Cuisine for some lunch." She smiles before squeezing my hands for reassurance.

I give her a small nod so she knows I'm okay before turning to Mitch and Jules. "Follow me." I begin heading out of the courtroom with them both hot on my tail, down the corridor and entering the first office on the left, I open the door for them both before I follow and close the door behind me.

Judge Donelly's office is warm and safe; family pictures on the wall along with medals and awards she's won, her desk facing the door and a khaki couch opposite. A beige wall theme with khaki decorative objects around the room, the room is perfectly leveled between dark and light. Windows surround each wall, apart from the one behind her desk, but its privacy is maintained, thanks to the cream blinds.

Jules takes a seat on the chair opposite the desk, with Mitch sitting on the couch. I debate whether to sit in Judge Donelly's chair, but Mitch looks at the empty space next to him and looks at me expectantly, so I take a seat on the couch.

I try to accept the silence, but honestly, it's putting me on edge. I know they're looking at me like I'm a helpless victim. I've been receiving that look for the past few days, and I'm getting sick of it.

I won't let *him* make me a helpless little lamb. I can cope with this and move on. He doesn't control me.

"Take it from the beginning." Jules says softly, giving me her undivided attention. "Every little detail counts."

*I can do this.*

Grounding myself, I close my eyes and take a deep breath. I tell my brain to focus on the facts, not my feelings. The thought of him doing this to someone else makes my eyes burn with hot tears. I can't allow that to happen.

"We were on a dinner date after meeting on the dating app At a Bar. His name was Chris, but I don't know if that's his real name or not. His dating photos looked like him but twenty years younger. He admitted he had those photos cleaned up."

Recounting the details makes it seem so fucking obvious that I got played, and for a moment, I feel sorry for myself. That makes a difference from the self hatred I've been feeling.

"I had cancelled on our date twice already, with work running over and I had a last minute doctor's appointment. He seemed okay with it and wasn't mad at all. His kindness was why I rescheduled. If he wasn't so understanding, I wouldn't have bothered, because we didn't instantly click. But the guilt of not pursuing anything forced me to reschedule, for the sake of my conscience." The words were a blur as they left my mouth.

"Take your time." Mitch's voice gives me a momentary distraction that I didn't realize I needed. I'm getting sucked into that place again and I'm terrified I won't be able to escape. "If you need a break, just let us know."

I nod, but I just want this over with, so I proceed. "We agreed to meet at The Rose Tavern for a meal so I got a cab over. He booked the table and told me the table number, which was eighteen, so I knew where he would be sitting. He was already at our table and as soon as I sat down, he poured me a glass of white wine which was already on our table.

"He was asking general questions and we spoke for a while about Casamount and how it's improved these past few years.

He told me he was a cop and he'd soon be a deputy with a promotion heading his way. I remember his statement made me tense up. I see a lot of cops at the courthouse, especially deputies, but I had never seen him before. With Casamount only having one police department, I thought maybe he was a transfer, but it didn't sit right with me. I congratulated him but I wanted to get out of there. He made me feel uneasy all of a sudden and I didn't feel safe, so I excused myself to go to the bathroom."

Suddenly, my throat feels tight and my voice feels like it's being strained. Flashbacks flood my memory and I'm back in that place, where he made me his puppet. This room feels like it's shrinking and I need to know I have space to move, so I rise to my feet and stand next to the window. I see the lock and I flick it and push it open, a cool gust of wind grounding me.

"My body felt wrong. I couldn't see properly, my head was throbbing and my muscles felt heavy. I couldn't hold my own weight and I could feel myself slipping out of consciousness. I knew something wasn't right because I only had one glass of wine. That's when I realized he drugged me. I'm assuming it was in my glass before I got there. I know better than to let a man I've never met pour my drink, but I was nervous and I was still trying to figure out who he was."

"It's not your fault, Saskia." Jules looks at me apologetically, her eyes soft and her voice gentle. "You can't blame yourself."

"I do." I shrug, but I push on. I don't want their pity. "I don't know if I passed out or caused a scene because everything went black. Not an ounce of my consciousness was working. I don't know where he took me, I don't know how long I was out for and I don't know what he did to me. The next thing I remembered was Mitch putting his jacket on me, my favorite black dress gone, and my head thumping so hard, I thought I was having an aneurysm."

I'm still waiting for that moment that sparks a flashback for me, but my mind is a black hole. There isn't a single thing I remember from the moment I passed out. I want to remember a place, a smell, anything. But it's just empty.

An upbeat ringtone cuts through the air, yanking me from the depths of despair. I look up, and Mitch and Jules are still looking at me like I'm a lost lamb. "Sorry about this, it's my kid's school." Jules looks between her phone and me, before shooting Mitch an apologetic look.

I'm not sure what she's apologizing for, so I wave her off. "Don't apologize. Your kids come first, go sort it." I smile, nodding at her so she knows I'm being serious.

"Are you sure?" She frowns, almost silently asking Mitch to ask her to stay. I know how this goes. They want both a male and female detective with a victim when taking their statement, so the victim is comfortable.

"Jules, it's fine, I promise." I say sternly. I know she won't take me seriously otherwise. "I trust him." I say, nodding my head towards Mitch but speaking to Jules. I know she sympathizes with me and wants to help, but I'd be always wanting to help my kids if I was a parent, too, so I don't blame her.

She nods and is out of the room quicker than a flash. I turn my body so I'm facing Mitch, now that it's just the two of us.

"You did great." He smiles, nodding at me. "Are there any distinct characteristics you remember about him? His accent, tattoos, scars?"

I put myself back at the table in The Rose Tavern and think back to my date. As I close my eyes and really focus, details start coming back to me. "His hair was graying, and long enough to fall behind his ears. Wrinkles, stubble, and a slight chip on his front tooth. A faded scar on the inside of his left wrist. He smelt of tobacco, earth and hay," I squint, trying to put my finger on the kind of scent I'm describing. "Kind of like a farm. A gold chain necklace and a raspy voice. His touch was calloused to my hand. Blue eyes, a left pierced ear. He used his hands to talk, but his right pinky finger was constantly bent, like he couldn't move it."

"Hey." Mitch's voice is soft, and I think I hear a hint of worry in it. "Sas." His hand is on my shoulder, and I almost flinch from the contact. I don't realize I'm still sitting with my eyes closed, thinking about my date until Mitch startles me. He pulls me out of a haunting daze and makes me focus on him. "You okay?" He questions, and I almost burst into tears at the soft way he's looking at me.

I can't find my voice because of the lump inside of my throat. I feel tears burning my lash line, but I try my hardest not to let them fall. Shaking my head, I meet his eyes. "Please find him." I plead, my voice barely above a whisper.

I don't miss the twitch on Mitch's jaw. It's clenched and visible, and for a moment, I swear I see his eyes darken. He doesn't seem focused on our conversation anymore, and is staring straight past me instead. "Mitch." I say, his eyes now meeting mine. "You okay?"

His composure comes in an instant, like he flips a switch and he's back to himself. "Yeah, all good." He nods. "It's not me you need to worry about."

His statement hits me like a stack of bricks. Pretending it never happened is working enough that I don't cry throughout the day, but as soon as someone brings the subject up, I want to bawl my eyes out. I just wish people would stop asking me about it.

"I think we've got everything. You did really well. I'll get this typed up and bring it by for you to read and sign. You've still got my card, right?" Mitch asks, his eyes focused on me. I nod. "Call me. Whenever you need, okay? I don't care if it's three in the morning, just call me when you need someone to talk to. Or not talk to."

Not talking can be the best option sometimes. It's reassuring to know he's there, but not exhausting to have to engage in a conversation.

I know I'll need therapy to get over this, but I'm just not ready to talk about it yet. Having Mitch on speed dial might be the best option for me right now.

A cop in my corner whenever I need him might be enough for me to fall asleep at night.

# 5

# MITCHELL

This case is going to test me beyond limits. I need to focus on the job. I've been doing this for ten years and I have always kept it professional and got the job done. There is a man out there raping and torturing women and I won't let that slide. He'll be brought to justice, one way or another.

But there's a problem. A five-foot-four, green eyed, Cuban problem. I shouldn't be getting distracted by her. I've met hundreds of beautiful women while doing my job, but they're just other women. Nothing more.

That's not Saskia.

Saskia is the woman I first saw in a courtroom a year ago and almost missed my stand call from a judge mid-trial. From that day onwards, I've not looked at another woman since. Saskia and her goddamn cherry necklace win my attention more than I care to admit.

Jules has teased and tested me, trying to encourage me to make the first move, and threatened me with dating apps when I refused, but I can't. Saskia's twenty-five, young and beautiful. There are men closer to her age that she should be going on dates with. Not a thirty-five year old detective, who can barely make it home before he gets called in again.

I should recuse myself from the case. It's a conflict of interest for me and I don't want to risk not getting justice for Saskia.

But I can't do that.

I won't.

I'll find that son of a bitch and show him what justice really is. Not the type of justice that's given in a courtroom, but the type that's given when the lights go out and there's no cameras for protection.

"Okay, gather round." Captain Wallace shouts as he enters the large office room. With white walls and brown desks, the decor is basic but it does the job. Desks are placed in twos, each one has a computer, phone and paperwork. Numerous whiteboards are dotted around with different case details on them and bulletin boards are placed within the gaps, with leaflets three years out of date pinned on them.

Standing at my desk, I head towards the large whiteboard at the end of the room with Jules following behind me. Photos of each victim are displayed with arrows trying to make connections, each photo is bullet pointed with important information, like name, age and ethnicity. Yet, the attacker still has a blank photo. We need to change that.

"Do we have an update on our attacker case?" Wallace proceeds, as the rest of the squad gathers around.

"We have units watching the storage location and the owner has agreed to give us access to the cameras within the building. We'll be notified if he returns. He probably has other locations to take his victims, because the crime scene unit found no evidence of other victims being ever there. He might not return, but we'll know if he does." Marten says as he flicks through his notes.

"Our perpetrator wiped their dating account but we've contacted At a Bar dating app and they've recovered our suspect's account." I add, walking up to the board and placing a piece of paper with a large question mark drawn onto it. "We tried to access his profile picture, but he has some sort of encryption on it. Tech are trying to crack the code. He goes by Chris, but we haven't been able to find him in any local or national databases. He probably used a fake name, which is why he uses actual photos of himself. Memorable details are a scar on his left wrist, a permanently bent pinky finger on his right hand. A chipped front tooth and an earring in his left ear."

Jules clears her throat before writing on the whiteboard. "We know his preferred locations to meet the girls are bars. Saskia is a different story, because he used a dating app to find her. He hasn't used that before, which means his M.O is changing or he's evolving. Saskia said in her statement that he smelled like hay and earth and that it reminded her of a farm. I'll look into local farm owners and see if anyone fits the description Saskia gave us. He's obviously local rather than transient so he could be a farm hand which would account for his strength. We also have been unable to track her phone. My guess is he has dumped it or thrown it in the river."

"He's aggressive and he likes to be in control. He takes his time to admire his own work and doesn't care for his victims during his torture session, but cares enough to drop his victim off near a casino once he's finished with them. He seemingly has no preferences, other than his victims being women. Age, race and body type are no issues for him. He sees women as a toy for his pleasure and will play with them until he's finished."

Hackett pitches in. "He makes himself wait at least twelve hours before he rapes his victims. Whether it's a sexual deprivation thing or he has other commitments, we don't know."

"Now, Saskia was a slip up on his usual perfect pattern. He's not had a victim get away before that we're aware of. We don't know how he'll react; whether he'll cut her loose and accept his loss, or whether he'll come back for her to finish the job." Marten's words are resounding and they cause my blood to boil. Knowing this pervert could be returning to finish the job on Saskia lights a poisonous rage inside of me. I want to protect her and fight for her. I'd even kill for her, if it came to it.

I can't hear anything other than my heart pounding. It thrums inside of me, each beat is a flashback to every crime scene I've attended in this case. I'm used to catching sick suspects, and I know how to turn off my feelings. But things are starting to blur together, and I'm not fucking okay with that. Not when it involves Saskia.

"Mitch?" Jules' voice is laced with concern as she pulls my attention from the board. I didn't even hear everyone else leave and return to their desks. "What's going on?" She presses, her eyebrows frowning and her eyes glued on mine.

"Nothing." I shake my head, pinching the bridge of my nose to regain composure. "I just want to catch this sick bastard."

The more I learn about this man, the more I struggle to grasp onto my sanity. Internally, I'm yelling my frustration at how he violated Saskia. He had no right to lay a finger on her, yet, he's taken what he wanted with no consideration.

Jules nods in understanding, her eyes falling on the board. Crime scene photos are dotted everywhere with notes and leads written around. It's an insight into a criminal's mind as we try to unravel their way of thinking. "How is she?" I don't miss Jules' not so subtle side eye.

I shrug. I don't know how to answer that. I'm not Saskia and I don't know how she's feeling. I've seen how she's coping, but how she really feels about being kidnapped? I don't think that'll ever come up in a conversation. "She seems okay. I gave her my card." I lean back on the table behind me, defeat slowly pulling me under.

"Has she used it?" Jules asks, copying my movements.

"Not yet." I scoff. "I don't think she will. She's pretty focused on pretending it never happened, but I wanted to give her the option. Being a victim can be lonely."

"If she needs you, she'll tell you, Mitch." Jules pushes off the table and steps closer to the board as she swaps a few photos around. "She trusts you."

"I know." I nod, rolling my sleeves halfway up my arms. "I just don't want her to lose herself. Not only has she got to deal with her experience, but her kidnapper is still out there. She's not going to feel safe until we find him." Fury and disappointment mix together in my stomach and make a dangerous cocktail of self hatred. I can barely pull my mind away from this case. I need to be able to tell Saskia she's safe and he's rotting in a jail cell.

But I can't.

Not yet, anyway.

There are units watching her home, day and night, for her protection. But I can't stop the twitch of jealousy burning inside of me. They are doing what I can't, and it irritates me.

I need to clear my mind and start fresh. I'm not going to be able to catch this man if my mind is too focused on Saskia. I settle for a coffee, a cold shower and a quick sparring session in the department gym.

Now, I'm ready to find this bastard.

# 6

## SASKIA

I'm not defenseless; it's mandatory to take self defence classes as an employee of the court. But I'm not exactly feeling safe and secure, right now. I'm constantly checking my surroundings, I jump at any slight sound, I'm eyeing up my exits. It's just a constant cycle of feeling like a target. I could handle it if he threw a punch at me. But nothing prepares you for being roofied on a date. How does someone prepare for that? It stripped me of all my senses; my logical thinking and my need to defend myself was completely wiped. It was in that exact moment, three seconds before I passed out, that I realized how defenseless I actually was.

The thought nauseates me.

The rape kit was negative, but no one knows what actually happened in the hours he held me captive, other than him. I don't know how exposed I was, what he did to me, if or how he violated me. Sometimes I think I was lucky that I was unconscious, so I don't have to remember what I went through, but I can't help but wonder if not knowing is just as bad. The evening plays on a torturing loop in my mind and there's no pause button to stop it.

I want to get back to my life, but I can barely make it to work without feeling unsafe. It's not like I feel any safer in my house, either. The police say to be vigilant so I find myself on edge 24/7. Knowing that I was found before he finished with me; it's a form of it's own torture.

It's hell living like this.

I need security. Safety. Peace.

Sighing, I shut my laptop and take a deep breath. My head naturally falls into my hands as defeat gets the better of me. Judge Donelly's office has always been a room where I can focus on typing up the day's court reports. Most of the time, the judge is in chambers or finished for the day, so I sit in my usual spot on the couch to do my type ups. But there's the odd time where she's in her office too, and even then, we sit in peaceful silence as we work.

But this past week has been different. I'm suddenly convinced the courthouse isn't safe. I'm constantly searching for some way he could get past security. Maybe in the public gallery, or a delivery man.

*Stop*.

I can't allow myself to think like this. Enough is enough.

Glancing at the clock on the wall in Judge Donelly's office, I watch as the hands hit seven o'clock. Accepting defeat, I shove my laptop into my bag and sling it over my shoulder, grabbing my keys and locking up the door behind me. My usual stroll home is going to be interrupted this evening for a last minute errand.

A hardware store.

🍒 • 🍒 • 🍒 • 🍒

God, I feel so out of place here. Out of all the people inside Casamount's Hardware Store right now, only one of them is female - me.I try to ignore their sideways lances and their lingering states, but it's hard when it's all you receive in male dominated locations. I dodge advances from low grade policemen and the usual low life on trial, but at least I feel somewhat safe within the courthouse. Here, I feel like a seal in shark infested waters, but I'm not going to let my fears stop me. It feels inevitable that one of these men is going to use me as prey.

The cool deep breath I suck in reminds me why I'm here. I hate feeling unsafe and I'm not letting Chris or any other man paralyze me with fear ever again. Mitch got my locks changed but I need something stronger, something I've chosen. So, I'm getting new locks for my front and back doors and I'm walking out of here, with my composure intact and my fists balled together. You know, just in case.

I quickly realize that I have no clue where to look, but there's no way in hell I'm asking anyone in here to help me. I'm not a damsel in distress. I can fend for myself.

Glancing at the store map, I search for the locks section. I head to section twenty-six, walking with my head held high down aisles, past the low grunts and whistles. The shelves upon shelves of different lock types scream at me as I gaze over them. Lucky for me, the description for each lock states which door it fits. I skim past the bathroom, garage, and gates section...until I find the selection of deadbolts. With so many options, I pick four of the strongest looking ones; two for the front door and two for the back. They look easy enough to fit, so I take them to the checkout and wait in the queue.

"Taking someone hostage?" The cashier laughs. His frail frame and grey mustache look like they're barely holding on. His glasses are so wide framed, his eyebrows fit into the lenses and his white hair has thinned to the point where I can see his whole scalp.

I want to tell him someone already did that to me but I don't want his pity, nor do I want the other men in the store seeing me as an easy target. So, instead, I laugh at his joke. "Something like that." I play along, my hand digging inside my purse for my card.

"Don't forget to rope their legs together!" He chuckles, sliding the metal over towards me.

My jaw clenches as I bite my tongue. Unwanted flashbacks assault my vision as my foggy memories force themselves to the forefront of my mind. My legs tied, rope burning my skin as I lay helpless and restrained. Nope! Not going there.

"Let's hope they're not yours." I deadpan, my glare set on him as I watch his smile suddenly drop. I want to laugh at his reaction, but I hold it in. Instead, I shove the deadbolts into my bag, trying to focus my attention on the present and not the chaos going on in my mind. My feet take me towards the exit, the fresh air already hitting my skin as I push the heavy metal door open.

I should have said more. I *would* have, but I already feel like I'm being watched. I don't need the extra attention from curious onlookers.

I can't keep falling into that fearful place.

I take a deep breath and close my eyes, centering myself. It's a ten minute walk from the hardware store to my home. Busy roads and lots of people. I can do this without being paranoid.

I focus on objects twenty-five yards in front of me to keep my brain occupied. Lamp post, fire hydrant, traffic lights. A couple sharing an ice-cream, keeping eye contact before they giggle at each other.

I catch myself smiling at their interaction, distracting me enough for a minute. Should I be worried at how easily distracted I am? No, I mean, it's what I was trying to do anyway, wasn't it?

I glance both ways before crossing the road, trying to focus on what's in front of me and not what's surrounding me. I subconsciously pick out the men in the corner of my eyes who look suspicious; black hoods covering their heads, hunched over, covering their identifiable features.

I shake my head and focus forward again. It's not him. He wouldn't risk it, would he? Out in the open, to drug me, no - too many witnesses. That thought alone reassures me.

Convincing me enough to keep my attention forward and not check over my shoulder.

Casamount is lively at all hours of the day, but especially in the evenings. Casamount keeps socializing alive; modern clubs, vibrant bars and a theme for all types of people. There's always an event going on that keeps money flowing and tourism alive. Casamount residents often disapprove of the nightlife, but if we didn't have the events, our city wouldn't be thriving like it is now.

Despite living in Casamount my whole life, I don't recognize a single person as I walk down the streets. The realization makes me feel uneasy. I don't know a single person here, which means there's not a single person in my corner. I don't know if they'd protect me. I don't even know if they'd stop and help me if I needed it.

Deep breaths, Sas.

I don't need help when I'm walking home. I've walked these streets a million times before and nothing has happened. This time will be the exact same.

One foot in front of the other, I see my red door as I walk down the uneven sidewalk. But unease fills me when I realize the police car isn't outside. They're supposed to be keeping watch of my house twenty-four-seven, but they aren't here.

Dread weighs my stomach down as nausea overcomes me. This doesn't feel right. I turn and check behind me, hoping to see the white and blue car driving down the street, but it's not there. Something much worse takes its place. I live on a quiet street with little to no activity, which is why he sticks out like a sore thumb. Black hoodie, no visible features and a large, hunched build walking towards me.

I gulp, fear almost paralyzing me on the spot. I could run into my house and lock the doors, but then I'm stuck in one spot. If he gets in, it's over for me. I need to be smart.

I need to fight for myself.

Screaming directions inside my mind over and over again, I start walking away from him, faster. I go to the one place I know I'll be safe and I pray to God I make it there.

My legs are weak, wobbling and burning with each step, but adrenaline pushes them through. I don't have the capacity to overthink right now. It's a somewhat pleasant break from letting my mind run through the endless bad scenarios I think about every night. Instead, I just focus on my surroundings. I need to get back to the main road. I need to be around people and I need to stay on route.

I don't want to do it, but I know I have to. Bile burns my throat as my danger radar blares in my ears. On the count of three, I check behind me.

One.

Two.

Three.

*Shit.* He's still there. Still following me with determination in his steps.

Panic lights a fire under me. Any logical thoughts that were going to appear are thrown like garbage. It's nothing but terror and hysteria in me now. Sweat beads on my hairline and my heart pounds in my chest, the speed making my throat burn as my mouth tastes of copper.

Dipping my hand into my pocket, I pull out the burner phone Mitch gave me. I pull his number up.

> On my way to the station. I think I'm being followed.

As I turn a corner onto the main road, I glance over my shoulder, but instantly regret it. He's closer now, his steps more aggressive and powerful.

I think I'm going to throw up.

> Where are you? I'm coming.

I try to reply, but my hands are shaking, so much so that I can't press the buttons properly. My body is itchy and my head thumps as anticipation keeps my adrenaline fired up. My body is fired up, giving me every warning it possibly can. And I hear it, but I can't think straight. I fight the tears that are starting to blur my vision as my body fights to keep going. My surroundings aren't clear as I pick out outlines of people, but no clear features. It feels like my odds are dropping quickly. I'm a mouse in a trap as a cat advances on me.

And I accept my fate as a hard force bumps me, making me stumble backwards. I fall into a hole of darkness as I realize he's going to finish what he started. Darkness closes in around me and I know there's nothing I can do about it.

"Hey." A firm shake of my shoulders pulls me back and as they steady me. "I got you. Take a deep breath."

*Mitch.*

"It's you." I choke, my tears carving a path down my cheeks. Like safety has formed a dome around me, Mitch pulls me close to his chest, the thrum of his heartbeat is even and hard against my head, each beat telling me I'm safe. "Thank God it's you." I can barely get my words out; the lump in my throat forcing me to swallow.

"Do you see him?" Mitch questions, keeping his hold on me, but letting go enough for me to turn around.

I dry my eyes enough for my vision to clear. I look for that black hoodie, but it's gone. Not a single person resembles him. "No." I shake my head, defeat engulfing me. "I panicked, I'm sorry." My body suddenly fights the heaviness that weighs me down. "The police weren't outside my house and everything suddenly felt wrong. I went to the only place I knew I'd be safe."

"You're safe with me, cereza." I soak in the heat radiating from Mitch's chest, his arms tense around my body. "Come with me." He coos, his arm looping around the back of me as he guides me around the back of the station. My hand instinctively touches my cherry necklace.

My legs burn from exhaustion as my adrenaline crashes. I stroll past the numerous police cars as we head towards Mitch's Range Rover. He guides me towards the passenger door and opens it for me, helping me into the seat. Shutting the door behind him, I hear him walk behind the car. I wait for him to open the driver's side door, but he doesn't. Instead, I see him in the wing mirror, on the phone. His words aren't clear, but his tone is angry.

The car door opens and Mitch hops in. "I just spoke to Wallace; the unit who were watching your house are being swapped out. The next ones will be better, I promise." His eyes are apologetic; soft and sorry.

"It's not your fault, Mitch. I'd be bored watching a house all day, too." I try to lighten the mood. I worry I just got someone in trouble, but my fear was valid. I'm on a never-ending ferris wheel of terror.

"It's their job, Sas. They *should* be keeping you safe." He releases a long sigh as he brushes his hand down his face. "I'd swap with them if I could."

I feign fake shock, my mouth falling open and my hand on heart. "Mitchell Alvarez doing a job that he wouldn't be addicted to? Full attention and phone recommended, but not required."

His laugh is soft and genuine. I watch as his cheeks lift and his eyebrows raise and I feel a smile on my face too.

Shaking his head, he swipes his tongue along his teeth, a smirk pulling at his cheeks. "Come on," he pushes the gear stick into drive. "Let's get you home."

# 7

## SASKIA

I don't believe in coincidences. Everything happens for a reason; whether it be a direct reasoning or an action to lead up to one big event, there's always a reason. But after the past couple weeks, my nonbelief of coincidences is beginning to wane. Two weeks ago, I'd see Mitch once a month in the exact same location, but now, I'm seeing him around three times a week. The circumstances aren't exactly great; statements, stalker updates, or *just* checking in, but I find comfort knowing he makes me feel safe. Probably down to the glock in his holster, but I can't find it in me to complain.

The five minute drive back to my place was peaceful. I found myself glancing out the window, looking for that faceless black hoodie, *hoping* I'd see him. Sometimes we need to face our demons head on, with our fear on our backs and our courage up our sleeves. Taking the step to bravery is a huge leap, but being able to put one foot in front of the other and feel the pride inside of yourself...that's empowerment. If standing up for what's right is what I need to do to put this sick man away, I'll do it like my life depends on it.

My home is dark and still, with no police sitting outside on patrol. I'm not shocked; it was the exact same twenty minutes ago. They couldn't bring in a watch team that quickly, even after Mitch gives them an earful. The sight is eerie; without human movement, my home is just a still shot. No activity and no personality. Just a still home, waiting for a human.

🍒 • 🍒 • 🍒 • 🍒

While the journey was only five minutes, it felt like it lasted forever. Hyper aware of every movement, I couldn't find a single thing to say. I already feel like an inconvenience to him, I don't want him to find me annoying, too. The damsel in distress who can't shut her mouth. Sounds like a mediocre Netflix show.

"Thank you for driving me home." I smile, grabbing my bag from the footwell.

"Anytime." He nods, his cheeks lifting as he meets my eyes. "You used my number." He nods.

"I'm a nuisance." Embarrassment heats my cheeks. "I won't panic next time."

"You're not a nuisance. You did exactly what I told you to do." His tone is softer now, and I can't help but believe what he says. "You can call me whenever you want."

Like a lightbulb has lit, an idea springs into my mind. "Would you mind helping me with something?" I flick my thumb towards my front door. "I need help installing a dead-bolt." I smile, my eyes darting away from Mitch's. "Or four."

Mitch chuckles gingerly, the sound calming me. I shake the feeling instantly. "Of course. Anything you need."

Before I can read into it, he's out of his seat and opening my car door. I unlock my front door, tip my purse upside down and let the deadbolts pile on the floor.

I separate them into two piles and I check the screws in the packet. "Let me grab a drill." I murmur, my mind focused on the screw sizes.

I head out the back door and open the large, metal toolbox. It creaks as I open it, the many items I've stored after doing DIY residing in here. Moving the paintbrushes and tester pots out the way, I spot the drill at the bottom along with the battery. Pulling it out, I hear some screws clank against the metal base. It's like a lightbulb flicks in my mind as an idea springs to me. The screws that come with the locks are so small, they'd barely put up a fight if a child attempted to kick down my door. I need more security. So, I reach to the bottom of the storage box and pull out a handful of screws. These look like they'll do a better job. At the very least they will give me time to call for help.

Shutting the box, my heart leaps a beat as the dark figure stands facing me. My hand instantly landing on my chest, in hopes of calming my thumping heart.

"It's me." Mitch coos, holding both hands up in defense. "You okay?" Concern paints a picture across his dark features.

"Yeah." I inhale a cool breath. "Sorry." My hand goes to my forehead as I slow my breathing.

"Don't apologize, cereza. I should have announced myself." He breathes a laugh under his breath, but I see his pinched brows and sunken eyes. He feels sorry for me.

"It's been a long day." I smile, but it doesn't quite reach my eyes. Instead, a pain behind my left eye becomes more obvious.

*Perfect, a stress migraine.*

Mitch's hands come out, flicking his fingers towards his body as he nods at the drill and screws in my hands. I pass the drill over and I drop the screws into his palm, and like a match has been struck across a hard surface, a hot flame is ignited between our touch. The electric charge shoots into my hand, awakening a feeling I'm not familiar with.

"Come on," Mitch nods towards my home, holding his hand out so I can go first.

*Always a gentleman.*

Silence gathers around us as Mitch works on the locks. I make sure they are all unwrapped and ready with their screws to make the job easier.

We work together in companionable silence, it feels comfortable in a way I've never felt before. "Will these make you feel safe?" He asks, his attention focused on fastening a screw. I can't see his face, but I hear the concern in his voice.

"Hope so." I shrug, watching over him. I hold my voice so he can't hear me falter. I need to sound sure for Mitch to believe me.

Mitch works on the final front door bolt. My eyes focus on the screw as it spins. His large hands as they fasten the metal. His tense biceps as they push against his thin sleeve.

*Damn.*

"Sas?"

"Hm?" Dragging my eyes away from his nice-to-look-at arms, I look at Mitch, his face confused as he smirks.

"Hold this for me." He passes the drill to me.

I grasp the handle, brushing his hand as I take it from him. *That igniting flame again.* An apology is on the tip of my tongue, but I notice that teasing smirk still on his lips, so I swallow my words. "Thank you for doing this. At least I'll have a fighting chance if I hear someone trying to get in."

I intended my statement as a joke, but Mitch's furrowed brows and wide eyes tell me it wasn't received that way. "Want me to stay a little longer?" He questions, testing the bolts.

I don't want to be a burden, but I also want to take advantage of the safety blanket Mitch offers. "If you wouldn't mind." I shrug. The adrenaline from earlier has definitely worn off, as my eyelids fight to stay open as the crash hits full force, my mouth constantly attempts to yawn and this migraine throbs against my skull.

"Come on, sit down." Mitch's hand on my lower back guides me towards the couch, but I protest.

"I have to do the back door ones." I throw my finger over my shoulder, my gaze looking towards the door. I'm trying to busy my mind to ignore the searing touch on my lower back as warmth curls within me. One slight touch from Mitch and my body is all reactive.

Shaking his head, he grasps the blanket on my couch. "I'll do them."

I sigh, unable to turn down his offer. Shaking my head, I can't stop the smile growing on my face. I sit down, as requested, and tuck myself under the blanket Mitch placed on my lap.

He flicks on the TV, unclips his gun harness and sits down beside me. It's mesmerizing watching him wind down. I only see Detective Alvarez, high alert and professional. Focused on his job of putting bad people away and saving those who need him. But this relaxed side to him is like peeling back a new layer. It makes me feel trusted; that he can rely on me to not use his weapon against him.

But as quickly as his calm demure arrived, it's going again, as the knock at my door is so hard, it vibrates my floorboards.

"Stay here." Mitch instructs, back in work mode, his hand instantly reaching for his gun.

I want to feel safe. I'm on the same side as the gun, but the sudden guilt feels like a pit in my stomach as I watch Mitch defend me. He always protects me, even if it means putting himself in the way of danger just to save me.

I can't help but wonder how far he'd go for the people he actually loved. Not just a slightly unstable sometimes colleague, like me.

The hinge clicks as the door opens, and all that built up fear is suddenly dissipated as Mitch breathes a sigh of relief. I hear him thank someone, but I don't see who, because my view is blocked by the huge bunch of red lilies.

He places them down in front of me, his cheeks tinged a slight pink as his eyes hover for a card. "Secret admirer?" He frowns, his demeanor suddenly on high alert. It doesn't need to be said out loud that this gift could be from my kidnapper.

I shrug. "Pretty intimate, considering they're my favorite flowers." My stomach turns, unease zapping my previous calm breathing into caution.

Forcing a deep, slow breath, I finally spot a tinge of white inside the green stems.

Relief washes through me as I see the name printed on the card.

"It's ok, they're from my best friend." A chuckle escapes my lips, my fingers pulling out the small slip.

*Don't die on me.*

*I like knowing your dating history is worse than mine.*

*Indie xx*

"Ouch." Mitch teases, his nose scrunching up. "At least she's honest."

"Painfully honest." I shake my head, placing the flowers onto the dining table. "Her's isn't much better."

"Sounds like she thinks it is." His raised eyebrows tell me he believes Indie, even slightly.

"Of course she would." I sit back down on the couch "No one admits how bad their dating life is. It's humbling."

Mitch smiles with his teeth, his perfect grin instantly forcing my cheeks to lift. "Hey, at least you have a dating life. The only woman I speak to regularly, out of work, is the woman at the gas station."

I squint. "Sounds like the opening to a romance book."

He smirks. "She's married to the man who stands right next to her at the till."

"Oh." My eyes widened. "So, you're into women who are taken, then?" I tease him.

His laugh is low but soft. It's mesmerizing. "No. I have respect." He surrenders his hands.

I laugh, and for a minute, I forget the intense pain behind my eye. But like a dart has been shot straight into my forehead, the pain is suddenly paralyzed. The lights are too bright, the television too loud. My stomach turns as nausea overtakes me.

"Hey," Mitch grabs the blanket and pulls it up to my chest. "Rest. You've had a long day."

I do as he tells me, letting my muscles relax and letting my eyes give in to the heaviness. I can't help but notice the gap between us. It's big enough to fit a pillow in between, yet I feel the heat radiating off him. Like he's electric, I feel his charge, zapping next to me like a current.

This is inappropriate. I can't think of him this way. He's working my case, therefore, he's a conflict of interest. I won't allow myself to fall into this trap and ruin either of our careers, I've worked so hard for mine.

Mitchel Alvarez is off limits.

And my consciousness can't bear to justify my actions as my mind goes dark, and every sound around me suddenly goes mute.

# 8

# MITCHELL

Rule number one of my job is to keep it professional. And that's exactly what I didn't do last night.

I'm an investigator on Saskia's case. I shouldn't be tempted by her, let alone visit her home for any other reason than discussing the case. Yet, there I was, fixing deadbolts and waiting for time to pass while she gave into her tiredness. That should have been my cue to leave; I'm no use when she's unconscious. Except, I didn't leave. I let her sleep on my shoulder, counting her deep breaths and listening to her slow heartbeat.

I could have left her to sleep on her couch and made my exit, but I couldn't leave it at that. I sat on her couch for an hour and it felt like sitting on a concrete slab. She'd wake up in pain, so I did the right thing and carried her to bed.

That was the perfect time to leave...except, I didn't. Her safety was the only thing on my mind, like I was convincing myself to find a reason to stay.

I can't lock the door from the outside and Saskia can't lock it from the inside when she's passed out. I don't like the thought of her being unconscious, home alone, with the doors unlocked, knowing there's someone after her.

So I spend the night on her ridiculously uncomfortable couch and sneak out before she wakes up. Late enough to hear she's awake, but early enough that she doesn't see I'm still there.

I double check there's a unit on patrol outside her home before I leave. I can't ignore the tug inside my chest as I think about her safety. It's an internal battle with myself; I need to put trust in those in a position to protect Saskia. But I won't truly accept she's safe until I see it with my own eyes.

*Boundaries, Mitch. Cases aren't personal.*

But Saskia is.

I have to bite my tongue as I pass the officers on patrol. Fury burns in my veins at the recollection of their absence last night, but I don't know for certain it was them who left their post.

I'm not interested in blaming others when it's not their fuck up. All I care about is they do their fucking job correctly, and Saskia is kept safe.

I offer a slight nod as I hop into my car, realization not hitting me until I shut my door. I'm not in the business of gossiping, but others are. If word gets back to my boss that I stayed over at a victims home, my job will be in jeopardy.

*Shit.*

Shifting the car into drive, I make my way to the station. At each stop sign, I attempt to call Jules, but nothing appears on my screen. Groaning, I toss it onto the passenger side as the battery symbol shows.

Time suddenly feels like it's of the essence. Each second leaves my heart palpitating with the acknowledgement of Captain Wallace finding out from someone who isn't me. My fourteen year career is flashing in front of my eyes. I've worked so hard to get here, I'm angry at myself for putting it at risk. I don't regret it though. Saskia's safety, Saskia's *life*, is more important.

Swinging my car into a parking space, I hop out and speed walk my way upstairs to Cap's office. I weave in and out of people with stacks of papers in their hands or a pile of evidence bags. Throwing meaningless apologies to those I bump into,

I set my eyes on Captain Wallace's office. My heart beats with each hurried step I take. Consequence and betrayal stir uneasiness inside of me. All the relationships, trust, bonds I've built at Casamount Police Department are suddenly so uncertain. I can't ignore the anxiety; I just need to clear this up.

"Where's Captain Wallace?" I gulp, my arms on the door frame to his office.

Sergeant Fields stares back at me, his gaze zoned in on my fast rising chest. "He's in the field this morning and then he's got a court appointment at three. Why?"

"I need to talk to him." My hand finds the back of my neck as I try to massage the stress building. "It's urgent."

"He has no phone in the field. Meet him at the courthouse at two-thirty, you can catch him before his appointment." Sergeant Fields flicks his eyes to his watch as he pours himself a black coffee.

I check my watch, frustration boiling inside of me. I have six hours to kill. Six whole hours waiting for someone to catch Captain Wallace before I do. Six whole hours of sitting on a confession that could cost my future.

I'm going to try and pretend my back isn't throbbing with a dull ache. I don't need physical pain added to my anxiety.

That's the shittest cocktail I've ever been served.

🍒 · 🍒 · 🍒 · 🍒

My body is erratic as I try to focus my mind on staying calm. Each step to the courthouse feels like a step closer to a bad decision, yet I know it's the right one. If I don't do this, I'll be putting Saskia's case in jeopardy. I'm not ruining her chance to get justice because I couldn't admit my wrong decisions.

Once I make it through security, I wait in the center of the main corridor. Each courtroom door is visible from here, so I'll be able to see Captain Wallace as soon as he enters. A brief text from Sergeant Fields to let me know Cap's appointment was brought forward, I mentally prepare myself to wait the extra time.

I don't notice my unease until my tapping foot catches the attention of a passerby. His side glance of disapproval is enough to make me stop, but it's not the loudness that bothers me. It's how agitated I am. Not only am I trained to do the right thing, I'm also trained to stay calm in all kinds of situations.

I need to be in control.

I need something to occupy my mind while I wait for time to pass.

*I wonder if she's here today.*

With no chance to reel it in, my brain finds a subject to distract itself. One that got me into this mess in the first place. I know her work hours, so she should be here. I guess I won't know until I see her.

God, I hope I see her.

My fist clenches, the shooting pain in my knuckles bringing me back to the present.

"Alvarez?" Captain Wallace's voice pulls my attention. His brows are pulled together as he tilts his head, confusion taking over.

"Cap," I step towards him. "I need to talk to you, urgently."

He nods towards an empty stairwell and begins walking. I waste no time following behind him. "What's up?" He asks, concern lacing his voice.

I wipe the sweat from my palms onto my legs as I swallow to hydrate my sudden dry throat. "There was an incident last night-"

"With the cops leaving their post at Saskia's? I know." Captain Wallace interrupts, disappointment clear in his heavy eyes.

"After that." I confirm. "She came to the station, had a panic attack, thought someone was following her. So I drove her home. She bought deadbolts for her doors. I helped her install them and I stayed with her afterwards, knowing there was no unit outside her house." I inhale a deep breath and maintain eye contact. "I lost track of time and I ended up sleeping on her couch. Nothing happened," I put my hands up in defence. "In all honesty, I couldn't leave in good conscience, knowing she'd have an unlocked house with no police watching her home. I'd never forgive myself for making her an easy target and not staying to protect her."

Relief lifts the weight of dread off my shoulders. Until Captain Wallace stares at me like I suddenly aimed a gun at him. The silence is starting to eat at me, and I have to fight every urge inside of me to say something. I open my mouth, hoping something, anything, will come out, but I'm abruptly stopped.

"Is that it?" Captain Wallace

My brows pull together as I recoil. Confusion makes me swallow my words as everything jumbles in my mind. "Yes?" I answer, unsure if that's even the right thing to say.

"Okay, come on. We need to head back to the station." His feet begin taking him towards the exit before I even get a chance to process what the fuck just happened.

"Cap." I raise my voice as I jog to catch up with him. "No punishment?" I squint. I can't work out if Captain Wallace is fucking with me, or if he's being serious.

"Punishment for what?" He looks left then right. His hand grasps my shoulder, pulling my ear towards his mouth. "You did the right thing, Mitch, watching out for her. We promised her twenty-four-hour protection, and we are expected to follow through with that. Those men on her watch last night will be disciplined accordingly, but when they stepped down, you stepped up. She's safe because of you."

She's safe because of *me*.

Not quite. It probably has something to do with her new collection of locks, but I like to think I helped.

"Come on." Captain Wallace claps my shoulders as he nods towards the exit.

It feels like the first opportunity I've had since this morning to breathe properly. Cool air assaults my lungs as I exit the courthouse doors, the slight chill leaving goosebumps on my exposed forearms. But as quickly as calamity came, it's stripped away, as chaos erupts in front of us.

Dozens of police attempt to contain the growing crowd as their protest signs and flags are held high. A calm protest isn't breaking any rules, which is why this current chaos shouldn't be happening. There was no violence or aggression from the protestors. Instead, it's from the brothers in blue. One-by-one, they pick off a protester and arrest them for some ridiculous reason. One side fights for their rights while the other fights for their desperate need to be in control.

But it doesn't last long when those who need control are faced with the unmanageable. That's when riots happen, and it's happening right in front of my eyes.

Fists are thrown, kicks are landed and handcuffs are secured tightly around wrists. Blood is decorated on cheeks, lips, heads, knees, each wound inflicted in an attempt to keep the situation contained.

My feet jog down the steps towards the crowds, my gun safely secured so it can't be used against me. I focus my eyes on civilians taking punches and still standing defenceless. The sight boils my blood.

But I wasn't prepared for the temperature my fury would rise to.

I can't stop my eyes from focusing on one person, the blood in my fists burning with the desire to put someone in their place.

I don't waste any time helping Captain Wallace de-escalate. Instead, I storm towards the left of the steps, my eyes never faltering. I see a commotion, and I silently pray I make it over there before anything happens.

Taupe business trousers, a black t-shirt and black heels. My eyes focus on body language, trying to pick up any cues. She's confused and angry; desperate to know what is happening to her.

I can't watch her distress any longer.

"Uncuff her." I growl, my voice low as my eyes lock onto the arresting officer. His uniform is a size too big and he purposely pushes his gun belt towards the front so it's in view. I have to take a deep breath to stop myself from punching this bastard right here.

"Mitch?" Saskia's voice wobbles. The way her brows pull together in confusion hurts my chest.

"You okay?" I ask, focusing my attention on her.

She shrugs, her lips barely lifting in a smile. "I was leaving work and I got arrested." She laughs, but it's humorless. "Great way to end the day."

Fuck this.

I get my badge out of my pocket and flash it to the cop. "Uncuff her. Now." My voice is barely above a whisper, but it's laced with venom. If he's smart, he'll see the rage stewing in my irises.

"I can't. It's my job and she was being disorderly." The cop shrugs like his life depends on this arrest. The way his shoulders are pushed back is enough to know he's proud of himself.

I can feel the fire burning in my stomach. I let out a breath before I take a step closer to him, the gap in between us now nearly non-existent. "I don't give a fuck if she was pointing a gun at you." My hand is itching to rope around his throat, but I compose myself. "Uncuff her, or I'll have your job."

His eyes are glued on mine, like he's trying to see me falter, but I don't do empty threats. There isn't an ounce of humor inside of me right now.

I see the challenge swimming in his eyes, but he complies. He unfastens Saskia's cuffs and places them back into his pocket. His mouth drops open to say something, but my gaze becomes like a burning flame. He'll be swallowing his words the second he directs them at Saskia.

"Thank you." Saskia murmurs, rubbing her wrists. I see the crimson marks around them, and the composure I had control over has suddenly obliterated. Saskia's injuries, the arrest, his refusal; it's enough to push me over the edge.

I turn around, my eyes set on the arresting officer. My mind is a constant flashing image of Saskia's wrists, each flash giving my anger another drive. I'm storming over, not caring who I barge into on my way over to him. But as quickly as I make the decision to punish him, the option is stripped from me.

A firm hand on my chest stops me. "Don't do it, Mitch." Captain Wallace hums. "He's not worth it. Get Saskia home. I'll speak to their commanding officer and ensure he's written up. The way this is going, they're all getting written up."

I can't budge the violent feeling sitting deep in my gut. He deserves to feel the pain and horror he put Saskia through. I *should* listen to Captain Wallace, but it's almost impossible when the devil on my shoulder is telling me to teach that pathetic officer a lesson. My ears throb as my blood pumps erratically, the sounds surrounding me fading away. My mind tells me to walk away but my heart won't let me.

I don't realize my back is tense until a soft hand is placed onto it. The touch is enough to pull me from this animalistic daze, I turn around to see who's behind me.

Saskia.

"Take me home, will you?" She raises one brow, a smile pulling at her right cheek.

All it took was for her to ask, and my anger suddenly disappears.

Fuck. What is happening to me?

"Come on." I nod towards the sidewalk, giving Captain Wallace a nod goodbye before walking Saskia to my car. It's a short two minute walk before my Range Rover comes into view. I open Saskia's door for her and close it after she hops in.

Ten minutes.

I have to make the ten minute drive to Saskia's home without thinking anything inappropriate. But the adrenaline infused blood pumping through my veins wants to head somewhere else. *No, ignore it, it will go away.* I can do that, I think.

"That was my first time being handcuffed." Saskia's nonchalant statement pulls me from my thoughts. I don't respond, because my mind is too fucking busy thinking about her being handcuffed. Restrained. Mine to play with.

*Stop.*

I clench my jaw, waiting for the shooting pain to distract me from my own thoughts.

"I mean arrested." She lets out a nervous laugh after she realizes what she said the first time, but the damage is already done. My mind is already creating its own seductive images of her cuffed and at my will.

"And it was for a crime you didn't commit." I respond, keeping my focus on the road. I take notice of the trees we pass and the cars we pass. The advertisements displayed on buildings and passers by, anything to distract me.

"I was worried I'd have to spend a night in the cells." I see her in the corner of my eye; her hands in her lap and her gaze focused out the window. My eyes dart to her direction as I watch her chest slowly rise and fall. I'm suddenly hyper-aware of every movement she makes. A slight jolt, a twitch, a deep breath.

"I wouldn't let that happen." I answer matter-of-factly.

Saskia turns her head to me, but I fight every nerve in my body to not turn to face her. I stay focused on the road, for my safety and for hers, but the temptation to glance over at her precious features is almost overwhelming.

Almost.

"Thank you for today." Her voice is soft. "I don't know what I would have done if you weren't there." She barely speaks loud enough for me to hear, but we're sitting in my car with the windows up. It's not hard to hear her whispers. *I wonder what those whispers would feel like against my skin.* Nope, not going there.

"You'd use your one call to call me so I could bail you out." I tease, my head turning to see her reaction. She breathes a laugh, her head shaking as she rolls her eyes. And it's at that exact moment I have to turn my attention to the road again, because her eye roll drives me insane.

I need a distraction. Anything to stop my mind from having free rein.

I settle for pain as I clench the steering wheel. My fists turn white as they throb from the pressure, but I don't let go. I can't.

I don't allow myself to release my grip when I see the patrol unit, and I don't release my grip when Saskia's house comes into view. I can't let myself falter yet.

"Thank you for this, Mitch." Saskia grabs her purse from the footwell as she grips onto the door handle. I silently curse myself for not opening it for her. "I owe you!" Shouts over her shoulder as she hops out of the seat. I watch her as she circles around the back of the car and digs her keys from her purse. She unlocks her front door and gives me a wave before heading inside.

And I release my solid grip from the wheel. Like a wave of cool air, relief washes over me. I can't get distracted, even when Saskia isn't here.

For the first time since she's entered my life, I'm thankful for her absence. But while she isn't here in physical form, she still dominates my mind. Her laugh, her voice, her curves.

The lingering scent of her perfume drives me crazy. They're innocent thoughts, until they aren't. I can't stop my mind from wandering to those red thoughts. The ones where she's laid bare, each inch of her delicate skin on display for me to admire. To touch. To taste.

*Fuck.*

*Control yourself, Mitch.*

The desire is too overwhelming. I can't fight it when my mind is the one tempting me down this dark path. I need it out of my system, so I can focus on my career and not Saskia Hernandez.

I pull up outside my apartment, wasting no time getting out. Fog clouds my mind as I'm set on one thing; easing the bulge in my pants. The desire is overwhelming and blurs out every reasonable thought within me.

Taking the stairs two at a time up to my apartment, I grab my keys from my pocket and force it into the lock. The door swings open before I can catch it; forcing me to shut it with less effort this time.

I pass my camel themed living room, the couches, curtains and rug all matching, before heading down the corridor to my bathroom. Black tiles with dull lighting give the most relaxing setting. This room is my favorite place when I've had a hard day at work. Calmness and serenity echoes off the walls, my body able to truly relax here.

Except, I can't relax when my dick is harder than steel right now.

I flick the shower on to lukewarm and undress myself before hopping in.

God, this feels sinful.

But I can't bring myself to stop.

My right hand finds my cock, hard and dripping in precum. A jolt of electricity shoots through my veins as my arousal controls me. Fat droplets of water assault my body as goosebumps appear on my bare skin. Pumping back and forth, I try to focus on my orgasm, but I can't control the dark desires in my mind.

*Saskia goddamn Hernandez.*

She infiltrated my mind and has taken over my every thought.

I grab the cherry scented body wash in front of me and open the lid. It was an impulse buy that left me feeling shameful after. I don't use cherry body wash, but I know she does. The scent clings to her skin and now it clings to my mind.

Each pump brings me closer to the edge, my senses on overdrive as I inhale the scent of the thick cherry liquid. My mind is red as I envision her golden skin exposed. Her pert nipples in my mouth as I suck and flick each one. Her soft gasps of surprise and her thick moans of pleasure. Her legs spread, her sweet pussy wet and ready for me.

God, I'd *devour* her.

My cock is painfully hard and begging for release as my balls twitch in reaction. Each pump is a blessing to reach my high and a punishment to only be able to imagine Saskia. I imagine it's her mouth around my cock, sucking and licking each inch of me. Her eyes pinned on mine as she takes my length, my dick touching the back of her throat. Every pump is a perfect image of me fucking her gorgeous mouth.

*Fuck.*

My climax edges me as my eyes shut and my mouth falls open. Like an open flame, my orgasm takes control of my suddenly weak body as limbs feel weightless. Hot cum drips from my cock as my body jolts, each pump emptying me. My eyes squeeze shut as stars begin appearing and my moans fall from my open mouth.

Slowing my pumps, I slowly open my eyes as my breathing returns to a calm rate. My legs feel weak, so I hold onto the wall as I collect myself.

Letting a deep sigh release, I focus on washing my body and getting myself cleaned up.

I've crossed a line, but it's only one I can see. Saskia may be a victim in my case, but before that, she was the woman I knew from court. I'm not justifying my own actions, I've stepped into dangerous territory, but now it's out of my system, those inappropriate thoughts should be exercised from my mind.

I fucking hope.

# 9

## SASKIA

Fear had its cold hands wrapped around my throat yesterday. The second I noticed a commotion outside the courthouse, I had a bad feeling. But, I thought walking past the large crowd wouldn't be an issue, especially when I'm not a part of it.

Oh, how wrong was I...

The moment that cop laid eyes on me, I knew things weren't going to go my way. He had this look in his eye that screamed corrupt dominance. He wanted to be in control so he could be the one to call the shots. It didn't matter to him that I wasn't involved; he did what he wanted to make himself and his career look good.

Except, it didn't end that way. I watched as his eyes went from control to belittlement as Mitch confronted him. Given, it wasn't handled the best way, but it got me out of the cuffs and I'm more than grateful for that.

The thought of a night in a prison cell makes my skin crawl. Metal beds, no bathrooms and a thin, torn blanket for cover; it's less than the bare minimum. I'd be safe from my stalker, at least.

I wouldn't be able to face Judge Donelly the next day, either. How would I explain to a judge of the court that I got arrested for protesting and spent the night in a cell, when it wasn't even me? It doesn't sound convincing in the slightest.

That's why I'm now walking up the stairs in the police station, carrying a six-pack. I pass officers on my way up and offer them a nod in greeting. I choose to ignore their side-eye when they notice the beer in my hand. You've got to be a brave kind of person, taking alcohol into the place where you can be arrested within the second. After yesterday, I know one person who would bail me out.

The butterflies in my stomach almost force a squeal from my lips, but I contain myself. I can't stop thinking about yesterday. About him. Mitch saved me and took me home; and while that should be a normal exchange, it feels different coming from him. It's like the high from stopping at the top of a ferris wheel; your surroundings just blur away. It's just you two, at the top, the world on pause.

I shouldn't let myself think these thoughts. Our relationship is strictly professional, not to mention crossing a line into dangerous territory. I know it's unethical and I shouldn't be enabling it, but my thoughts are for my eyes only. He makes me feel safe, and that's something I'm seriously lacking in life lately. I can allow myself to indulge without actually indulging physically.

Finally making it up the stairs, I spot the occupied desks in front of me. My eyes scan the room, but I sigh when I can't spot Mitch. I take in the whiteboard to my left with case information displayed on it. I wonder if I have one of those. Shaking my head, I focus back on the room; white walls, brown desks and wheely chairs...it looks more like a staff room than a police department.

With people on their feet and attending to their duties, I feel almost invisible. Maybe Mitch has the day off today? I can't even figure out which one is his desk. Sighing, I pull out my phone to shoot him a text, but a black ponytail catches my attention.

"Jules," I wave my hand to grasp her attention.

She hops out of her desk seat and walks over to me, a smile plastered on her face. "Hey Saskia!" She hugs me. "Looking for Mitch?" She squints at me like she's in on some secret, but I choose to ignore it. I don't know what she's implying and I'm not going to indulge in it right now.

"Yes," I nod. "Is he here?"

"Mmhm." Jules points towards the closed office to my right. "He's in Captain Wallace's office doing paperwork. Go knock, he'll be happy to see you." She smiles, raising her brows before walking back to her desk.

I get the feeling she wants me to know she has knowledge of a big secret. I just don't know what it is, and I'm not entirely sure Jules does either.

Walking towards the closed door, I rap lightly on the glass and wait for a response. I faintly hear a 'come in' so I open the door enough to peek my head in. "Hey." I smile, my eyes instantly meeting Mitch's as he sits at Captain Wallace's desk. "Can I interrupt?"

With one hand wrapped around a pen and the other on his head, his head rises and his cheeks lift, showing that perfectly white smile. "Hey." He stands to his feet, wasting no time walking over and opening the door fully for me. "Yeah, come in." He waves me in and shuts the door behind me, leaning against the desk. He's wearing his usual white shirt, with the sleeves rolled up and grey slacks. *He looks good.*

"These are for you." I pass over the six-pack of beers and wait for him to grasp them before taking a few steps to my left. Leaning back on the cupboards behind me, I try to focus my mind on anything other than his taut forearms pressed against the table. "They're just a thank you for saving me from a night in lockup." I breathe a laugh.

His hands brush past mine as he grasps the beers, and I swear I feel a zap of electricity. I immediately put my hands behind my back. "You don't have to thank me, Sas. I'd do it again if it comes to it." His lips lift in a crooked smile, his eyes pinned on me.

I suddenly feel warm in this room as sweat threatens to gather on my hairline. All the blinds are down and windows closed making it a hot box, but that isn't why I feel hot. I take a deep breath and attempt to compose myself.

God, this is embarrassing.

"I'll try not to make it a habit." I tease. "Same with the locks." I joke, rolling my eyes.

He laughs out loud, and I have to fight my muscles to not melt on the spot. "How are they holding up? I heard your handyman is pretty good at his job."

"They are holding up perfectly." I nod in assurance. "He deserves a raise."

His brows shoot up in surprise. "A raise, huh?" His gaze alone is enough to make my breathing faster. It's embarrassing that I have to remind myself to take deep breaths. "He sounds great."

"He's kind of been my knight in shining armor lately." I scrunch my nose as I try to contain my smile, but I want to swallow my words as soon as they leave my lips. I panic that I've gone too far, too deep into the conversation. I can't retract my words when they've already left my lips.

Mitch's mouth falls open to say something, but a sudden blaring bell echoes next to my ear. I can't see where it's coming from, but I can hear that it's on top of the cabinets I'm leaning on. I turn to take a look, in hopes to turn off the sound, but my body freezes its movements. Sandalwood and mint with a hint of cherry invade my nostrils as Mitch's arm reaches past my face and to the alarm.

I'm suddenly hyper aware of how close we are. His body is mere inches from mine as he reaches above the cabinet to get the alarm clock. "Sorry." He hums, his arm coming down to his side with the alarm clock in it. "It's to remind me to have a break." He shrugs it off, but I can barely register his words. I'm too focused on the small gap in between us.

I meet his eyes as I lift my chin, his large figure standing over mine. My breathing is suddenly twice as fast as it was before. It's like we are both frozen in this position, neither of us wanting to back away but we can't go forward either.

I can feel the heat radiating from his toned body, his muscles visible through his shirt when I'm this close to him. I see his stubble growing back, his throat bobbing as he swallows. How inviting his lips look.

Stepping away is what I should be doing, but I can't get my feet to move. I can feel the thick tension between us as Mitch takes a step closer and closes the gap. His body is pressed against mine, and his heart is thrumming in his chest wall as it vibrates onto my skin. Warm hands find my cheeks as Mitch grabs my face, his lips grazing over mine as he teases me oh so painfully.

"We shouldn't be doing this." He whispers, his breath hot against my skin.

"I know." I agree, my words barely audible but desperate.

It's torture waiting to see how this plays out. His lips are on mine, but neither of us have given in. I want to taste him. Touch him. Learn how he kisses.

"Fuck it." The words leave Mitch's mouth breathless, and I don't get much time to process what he said before his lips crash against mine. A lit match meeting gasoline, my whole body erupts as we both give in to temptation. It's hot and wet, each kiss leaving me panting but in desperate need for more.

His hands are in my hair and my hands are on his back. It's passion and chaos mixed together as the world fades away around us.

Until, a loud knock at the door snaps us back to reality. Mitch pulls away as my hands find my curls, finger brushing them in an attempt to tame the wildness they've become. The door opens with a click and Jules pops her head in. "Can I go over these with you?" She questions while looking at Mitch, holding up a stack of papers.

"I was just leaving." I straighten out my coat before heading towards the door. "Bye!" I offer a quick wave over my shoulder, but I don't waste time with pleasantries. I need to get out of there and breathe actual air that hasn't been saturated by Mitchell Alvarez.

Trusting an Uber to drop me home so my stalker doesn't corner me was the safest way, but my safety wasn't my concern, for once. Instead, my mind was a series of flashbacks of five minutes before. I can't focus my mind on anything other than the earth shattering kiss I just had.

I know it's wrong. I shouldn't even be thinking about going there and I don't want Mitch to get fired. I could never forgive myself if his career was ruined because of me. He doesn't deserve that.

Yet, sometimes connections are hard to ignore when they're looped around your limbs. I know the difference between a working relationship and a personal one. He's the reason I know the difference. We've crossed the professional line and are tiptoeing on warnings.

But his career means more than a kiss. This is his livelihood. Everything he's worked for. And I'm not going to put my own selfish needs first, especially when there's so much at risk. I've ignored many criminals who sit opposite me in the courtroom. I can ignore my feelings, too.

Frustration claws at my insides as I lay in bed, staring at the dull ceiling, letting myself sink into a pit of sorrow. The more I tell myself Mitch is off limits, the more my brain replays the kiss. The tension and passion could have created enough electricity to light the eastern seaboard. Lust and liquid desire lit up my insides with each touch he placed onto my body.

My thighs dampen at the thought.

*Shit.*

As a deep sigh escapes my lips, I reach into my top drawer and pull out my ruby red vibrator. I lower my panties and flick the on switch as I guide the toy to my clit.

My legs instantly open in response. High intensity pulses tease my pussy as my free hand finds my breast. Squeezing and pinching my nipple, soft moans escape my lips as the blissful feeling engulfs me.

Like a movie, my brain replays Mitch's hands in my hair, his wet lips on mine. The way his eyes drank me in with each glance. I let my mind run free, taking itself down whatever dark path it desires.

I wonder how he fucks. If he's soft and reassuring or if he's rough and passionate. I wonder what he tastes like. How my pussy would swallow his cock as he thrusts into me. I wonder what his moans sound like.

My arousal builds between my legs as the vibrations intensify. Erotic visions take over as my orgasm builds. Each vibration is a new image of the man who's been protecting me these last few weeks. I can't stop my back from arching as my muscles contract and my legs spread further, my high seconds away from taking over.

It's ecstasy taking control of me; my body feeling weightless as my vision turns black. My fist clenches the bed cover as my other can barely hold the vibrator against my throbbing clit. I can't stop my body from shaking as my moans become louder. Biting my lip, I ride my high until my body lays lifeless from the mind blowing orgasm I just experienced.

Reality sets in, shame weighing my chest down as I accept what I just did. My body is frozen in shock; my eyes wide as I sit up and glare at the wall opposite me.

I can *never* touch myself while thinking of Mitchell Alvarez ever again.

# 10

# MITCHELL

"What's gotten into you?" Jules' tone is playful as she lightly punches my arm, mischief swirling in her eyes.

There was another victim last night. She was dropped off at a casino, unconscious and undressed. Burns from what we believe is a cattle prod mar her skin, with several restraint marks on her wrists, legs, and across her mouth. The victim barely said anything when we picked her up, thanks to the high levels of sedation drugs in her system, but she did say a location. Whether it's where our suspect is or if it was just a location she remembers from last night, we waste no time following it up.

Our suspect may be good at covering his tracks and keeping himself hidden, but I don't give up. I'll play the long game if I have to; there isn't a single case I've worked on that has been left unsolved. Cold cases aren't an option. And closure shouldn't be a luxury. It's a necessity.

"What do you mean?" I counter, fastening my bulletproof vest so it hugs my chest tightly.

A run down motel that's on its last legs stands in front of us, with rotten wood for roofing and chipped paintwork for an exterior. The motel doors were red a long time ago, but now they're a dull brown, with specks of red that look like blood splatter. Ice machines are dotted on the bottom floor with flies using them as a breeding ground and vending machines have shattered glass for windows.

The *Mill Lane Motel* sign is hanging off and some of the neon letters have blown leaving it displaying 'ill Motel'. Looking at the current condition of this place, the illuminated name seems fitting. The city building inspectors need to take a trip up here sometime soon.

"You seem distracted." Jules slots a spare magazine into her back pocket and hands one over to me. "What's on your mind?"

A deep sigh slips past my lips. *Who, not what.* I can't stop thinking about that kiss. It was a flame of desire and tension looped into one. Saskia was a lit match and I was gasoline, anticipation thick as we hovered in front of each other, but didn't touch. The moment I closed the gap between us, it felt like an eruption of chaos shooting through my veins. Knowing I shouldn't be kissing her perfect lips made the adrenaline rush damn near impossible to resist. There's something addicting about her presence; I won't be beating that addiction any time soon. I can't. Not when she occupies every inch of my mind and dominates my thoughts.

"Just this case," I sigh, rubbing my hand down my face. "It's ruining peoples lives and I'm losing my patience."

"I'm with you." Jules places her hand on my back and pats it a couple times. I feel the support through her sympathetic smile. "We'll get him sooner or later, and you can stop worrying about Saskia's safety."

I shoot her a side glance and I *hate* the smirk that's looking back at me. Like Jules knows something she shouldn't. "Don't worry, your secret is safe with me."

"I don't have a secret." I shrug it off, checking my phone in my pocket for any notifications, just for the distraction.

"Oh, okay." Jules shrugs, looking around her before proceeding. "So you kissing one of our case victims isn't a secret? I'll let Cap-"

"Enough." I grunt through my clenched jaw. "I had a lapse in judgement. It won't happen again." The words leave my mouth before I can admit them with certainty, but I'm not prepared to tell Jules that. She's been my partner for ten years and I trust her with my life, but she's like a sister to me, and she loves to tease me like we're siblings. I'm not giving her that ammunition.

"I don't believe that for a second." Her response is instant, but barely a whisper. "I don't know if Cap would approve, but I can see why you're both drawn to each other." I frown, barely offering Jules a side eye as I wait for her to continue, but when she stares off into the distance, I move my hand in circles to get her to finish her damn sentence. "She feels safe when she's with you. You aren't so broody when you're with her. It's like you balance each other out. You take away her anxiety and she takes away your grumpiness."

I let out a snort. "I'm not grumpy." My face screws up instinctively, but my mind is too focused on the warm feeling inside of me. One sentence, five words. *You balance each other out.* An explosion of feelings burns inside of me.

"That's what you took away from that?" She rolls her eyes and throws her arms up in defeat.

"I listened to every word." Like a hushed confession, the words barely make it out. But my admission doesn't go unnoticed. I see Jules' side glance, but she doesn't have time to react as Captain Wallace's voice draws our attention.

"We have officers at the rear of the motel; we're going in from the front. Watch each other's sixes and stay focused. We need stealth and composure." Strapped in tactical gear, we approach the motel. In twos, we each take a room, looking out for anything suspicious. This is our only lead right now, we aren't wasting any time following it up.

Impatiently waiting for Captain Wallace's go ahead call through the radio, I have Jules behind me with her gun raised, ready to take action. Like the beginning of a race, as soon as the countdown is called, my foot meets rotten wood and kicks open the motel door. I'm met with a couple, both drunk from the empty vodka bottles dotted around the floor, taking part in what I can only assume is sex. Neither fit the description, so we move on.

The second, third, and fourth rooms were empty; none looking used but not particularly clean either. Crime scene investigators will comb through this place once we're done; we're just locating anyone who could be of help.

Door five has a busted lock, so I save my foot the trouble and push it open with my shoulder. A fifty year old country looking man lays with a lit cigar hanging out of his mouth, watching some sort of old western movie. He's not our suspect, but he's definitely suspicious of something. The white powder on the side table is enough evidence.

I accept our loss and move onto room six. The room smells musty from the outside, like it hasn't seen a hoover since the nineties. The windows are covered in smudge marks and the curtains are closed, displaying their off yellow color from the constant use of cigarette smoke.

Giving Jules a ready nod, we breach the property and begin searching. The room is dark, the only accessible light is from the door I just kicked in, illuminating the dirty walls. The bed has no bedding on it and there's no other furniture in this room. There's a strong smell of bleach attacking my nostrils as I head to clear the bathroom. The toilet water is about to overflow and the sink and bath are both full up with dirty water. Sewage scent wafts around the small room as I notice the flies around the toilet brush.

"All clear." I shout to Jules, fighting my body to stop it from dry heaving. That bathroom itself should be a crime scene.

"All clear." Jules confirms behind me, brushing a stray hair behind her ear. "I'm going to grab a notepad and question that guy next door."

I nod, heading outside for a breath of fresh air. There's something about this room that screams skeptical. I don't like how the bathroom is a hazard from the smell and mess, yet the main room smells of undiluted bleach. It's the best way to destroy evidence, but the scent bleach leaves behind is a clear sign that something was cleaned up in here.

Leaning forward, I look closely at the bed frame and see if I can spot any hairs or fibers that have been left behind. Any shred of evidence in this room needs to be collected and tested. I'm not losing this asshole again.

Jules' footsteps come in behind me, but I'm too focused on the small white object in front of me. Sitting on the bedside table is what appears to be an adult tooth. I grab a scene marker and place it next to it. When the scene techs come in, they will process it. The temptation to pick it up is overwhelming. Something this small could give us the next step in our case.

"Hey, come look at this." I call behind me, my eyes glued on the tooth.

I don't hear Jules come closer, but I definitely heard her come in. "Jules." I call out to her again, but she ignores me, like I'm not even in the room.

Recoiling, irritation sits at the forefront of my mind as I turn my body around to face her, so I can see what has her so distracted. But the second my body turns, my eyes meet with green ones, only visible through small holes on the face mask they're wearing. We silently assess each other for what feels like an eternity, my brain trained to take in every detail, but in reality it was only long enough for him to raise his gun and shoot.

Blistering pain shoots through my shoulder as the bullet enters my flesh, the hit forcing me back against the bed frame, as two questions float across my mind before I black out; what if this person has hurt Jules? What if this is the person who hurt Saskia?

I tell myself to apply pressure and defend myself, but I don't get the chance as my vision is obliterated. Like a brick has pounded against my skull, my vision is spotty as my eardrums thud, my consciousness slipping into darkness.

Distant voices pull me from my sleeping state as my senses begin awakening. I can hear beeping, footsteps and hushed voices mentioning my name, but I can't piece together their words. Forcing my fatigued eyes to open, my vision is blurry as it adjusts to the overhead light shining above me. The bulb is long and thin, like one you'd find in a hospital.

Shit.

I'm in the hospital.

A flood of memories assault my mind as I remember where I was and what I was doing. I remember the masked man. I remember the bullet entering me. I remember hitting my head against the frame. And then I remember the tooth and the realization of how unsafe Jules and Saskia now are.

I sit up in one quick jolt; tubes in my arms moving with me, blindly searching for my phone, but the sudden motion makes the room swim. Whatever they've got in that drip is strong.

Looking down at my wound, I assess my injury. I'm shirtless, with spots of dried blood decorating my skin. My bullet wound is now a closed wound, with stitches holding together the injury site. Checking I still have mobility, I carefully move my right arm. It hurts like a bitch, but everything still works. A sigh of relief feels like a weight is lifted from me.

"You're awake!" Jules' voice is a wash of comfort as she enters the room. She looks like she hasn't slept in twenty-four hours; with dark circles under her eyes and her hair in a loose ponytail that's barely holding. She practically runs over to the side of my bed, her hands buzzing to find mine. "Please don't ever scare me like that again."

It's the first time I've seen pure fear swimming in her eyes. "Sorry." I shrug, letting a small laugh slip my lips, but instantly stopping when the movement hurts my chest. "I don't know who it was, Jules." The confession burns my tongue as it leaves my mouth. I feel like I have a target on my back now.

"Did you see who shot you? I was in the room next door when I heard you go down. It's like whoever shot you knew we were going to be there, or..."

"Jules!" I shake my head, she can't verbalize what I've been thinking, not here. "He was a white male, similar height to me, black hoodie and trousers, black mask and green eyes. I didn't get a look at the gun he used, but I think it was silver and he used a silencer."

"Ok, I'll put a BOLO out for anyone matching that description. We'll have every cop in the city looking for him." The words leave her lips with urgency, but she stops as soon as my eyes widen. "Well, apart from the cops watching over Saskia."

Thank fuck.

"There is a slight problem." Jules winces, her eyes tightening as she looks at me sympathetically. "When I found you in a heap on the ground, your holster was empty Mitch - your gun was gone." Her face looks defeated, like she already knows the answer to her question. "Did you put your gun down anywhere? A safe space maybe?"

My left hand brushes down my face as I compose my frustration. "It was in my holster, Jules. That bastard must've taken it."

"I thought that may be the case. I'm going to call it in." Jules nods as she slips through the sea blue curtains.

Fury itches my veins. That prick not only shot me, but he took my gun. He passed a dozen officers without getting caught, so he's familiar with the area. Possibly even targeted me or our squad.

"Mitch," Jules pops her head back in through the curtain. "Anything you want to say to Saskia-"

"I don't know," I groan, my body aching. "That I need mouth to mouth, maybe." The words slip my lips before my brain has time to stop it.

"Behave, Detective Alvarez." The soft voice pulls me from my thoughts as my gaze shoots to the moving curtain. Saskia slips in as Jules slips out, that mesmerizing playful smile on her lips. She's dressed in cream work pants and a black t-shirt tucked into her waistband. "Thank God you're okay." Her words come out as more of a question than a statement as she focuses her attention on my wound. Her breathing quickens and her eyes widen as she assesses my bloodied and bruised skin.

I want the ground to swallow me whole. I wasn't expecting her to be here, let alone enter my hospital room. Jules could have given me some sort of warning before I made a dick of myself. "Sorry." I shake my head, trying to come up with some sort of excuse, but I don't have one. "I'm okay." I nod, unable to stop my cheeks from pulling up. I never noticed it before, but there's a small, red, cherry tattoo on her left bicep. It's delicate, but it's *her*.

"Jules called and let me know what happened." Those gorgeous brown eyes are pinned on me, and I suddenly feel like I'm being studied. "Judge Donelly dropped me here." She lets a laugh slip her perfect lips, but the humor isn't there. Her voice drops a decibel and her brows pull together. "You scared me."

*Fuck.*

"I'm sorry, cereza. It won't happen again." I promise her, although I'm not sure I mean it. My job comes with risks, and getting shot is one of them. My hand finds hers, our skin gently touching before she lightly grips mine. My thumb instinctively rubs circles on the top of her hand. "You didn't have to come." I reassure her.

"I wanted to." She smiles, her gaze quickly flicking between my stats machine, back to me. "Do you need anything? Mouth to mouth?" She teases.

"Well, now mouth to mouth is on the table," I can't stop the chuckle escaping my lips but the movement makes me wince. "A drink of water, please."

"Captain Wallace is out there, I'll see if he's up to it." She jokes, grabbing the full cup of water on the bedside table and handing it to me. "I would offer," she shrugs, rolling her eyes, "but I was told we shouldn't be doing...that." She draws out the final word as she implies kissing.

"Glad to know Cap gets a free pass." I tease. She consumes me; each word that leaves her lips have me mesmerized by all things Saskia Hernandez. "I'll let him know he's on standby until I get released in a couple days."

"Well," she smiles. "I'll come check on you each day so you don't lose the will to live."

"Something to look forward to," I smirk. "It'll keep me sane until I'm out of here."

Fuck. I can't help but flirt with her. She brings out this side of me that feels like a teenage boy. The flirting, the teasing, the tension. The need to know everything about her. Her fears, her dreams, her goals. I want to know *everything*. It controls me. Pulls me about like a puppet.

But then I'm faced with the reality that I'm out of service for a few days. I'm restricted to this building under observation, while Saskia is out there, with a stalker on the loose. My jaw clenches as defeat gets the best of me. I'm useless to her, and I'll never forgive myself if something happens to her.

Grabbing my phone from the side table, I pull up Judge Donelly's number.

> I'm off duty for a couple days. Can't keep an eye on Sas. If she has any type ups to do, send her to my hospital room. I can keep her safe here.

> No reporting on her schedule for the next three days. Only type ups. She's all yours. You owe me, Alvarez.

I owe her a fuck load, now. Saskia has no cases to report. The only work available to her is writing up case reports. Which, with a bit of persuading, she can complete right here, in my hospital room. Where there's security, a bunch of staff, and a place I can keep an eye out for her.

She's all mine, indeed.

# 11

# SASKIA

I know Judge Donelly and Mitch have planned something. Never, in my four years as a court reporter, have I spent three days on type ups. I'm typing up court reports that aren't even mine, just so I can spend the days Mitch spends in hospital with him. I should be annoyed that they went behind my back, but instead, I'm thankful for their secret deliberation.

I was annoyed at first. I'm comfortable in the courthouse. When Mitch told me I'd be spending each day here in the hospital, instead of at work, being ferried between here and home by officers, all so he can know I'm safe. I refused. It was the first time I felt angry with him. But he didn't give up. He was stern and convincing, yet gentle in how he spoke to me.

It didn't take me long to realize it was for my safety. I know I can depend on him, because I know he's got my back, but he can't be much help in a hospital bed, so working from his hospital room was the logical option. He's resting and able to stay relaxed knowing I'm here with him the majority of the time, and I'm still working, albeit doing someone else's job, but it's still work. And I have Mitch by my side, somehow still keeping me safe, even though he's out of action.

Mitch has spent the majority of his time in the hospital asleep, his pain medication makes him drowsy. So I've been able to complete my type ups with time to spare. After his three day stay, he was finally released back to his own apartment, under the condition to not do any strenuous activities and to take a few more days off work. He begrudgingly agreed, although I don't trust he'll listen to the doctor's advice. He misses his job, and it's making him agitated. He's not coping well with being cooped up either. I don't think he likes knowing he can't help anyone.

So, I've made him a ropa vieja dish to hopefully take his mind off being on house arrest. It's the dish my Abuela would make whenever I was sick, so, I'm making it in hopes it will make Mitch feel better, too.

I catch an Uber to his apartment building, ten minutes from my home. Thanking the driver, I hop out with my glass dish in hand and head to the main door. It's locked and I don't have a key, so I pull my phone from my pocket and pull up Jules' phone number. But before I can press dial, someone exits the building and holds the door open for me. I offer them a smile before making my way up the stairs to the second floor. I look out for door number four, before knocking.

The sudden onset of anxiety begins gnawing at my stomach as I wait in silence. What if he's busy and I'm interrupting? Or what if he's not home? He has to be. What if he's with someone else? I gulp as nausea swirls my stomach. I try to distract my mind from the sudden jealousy that shouldn't even be present, but my mind won't budge. I can't budge the thought of him being vulnerable with another woman.

The sudden urge to scream is too strong to contain. The sound is on the tip of my tongue, but it dissipates the second the door opens in front of me.

Mitch is shirtless, his chiselled abs practically carved from the gods, yanking my attention. "Sas?"

"Hm?" Forcing my eyes to meet his, I try to focus on his face and not the perfection below it. He has bruises on his left temple and eye, with a small cut. His gunshot wound is still stitched nicely on his shoulder and the rest of the damage is barely evident anymore.

He squints at me, his head tilting to the side. "Come in." He nods towards his apartment, and steps back, allowing me to enter.

I follow him in, my eyes focusing on the decor. There's something telling about how a man furnishes his home. It's a camel color theme which works well with the dark gray pillows and small pieces of decor. There's a blanket on the sofa which is where he must be sleeping at the moment, with a stack of pills on the center table.

A pile of case files are next to the pills, which catch my eye. "Shouldn't you be taking some time off?" I question, my eyes bouncing between him and the files.

"From strenuous activities." He confirms, looking at me like I'm being told off. "Reading is as calm as I can possibly be."

"I'll let you off." I tease. I study his open plan design, my eyes focusing on his kitchen in the left corner. "I brought you some food to reheat, if you're hungry." I hold up the dish before walking towards the fridge.

"Eres un ángel." He walks over to inspect the food. After a long inhale, he closes his eyes and lets out a throaty moan. "Ropa vieja?"

I nod, but I'm still focused on how sexual his moan sounded. My heart suddenly begins pounding as I instinctively clench my thighs, missing whatever Mitch says next. "Hm?" I look at him, hoping he doesn't pick up on the sudden burning on my cheeks.

"Will you stay and eat with me, cereza?" He asks, preheating the oven.

"Of course." I agree, in hope I can get a handle on the red room thoughts buzzing through my mind. "You sit and I'll make the food." I try to say sternly, but the way he's looking down at me makes my stomach flip.

I watch his eyes graze my body before meeting my eyes. He reluctantly agrees before sitting on the sofa and putting a shirt on, letting it flow over his gray joggers. I can't help but feel defeated.

Is it acceptable to ask him to take it off again? You know, for healing reasons. Stitches can't heal properly when covered.

Placing the food in the oven, I pull out some plates and cutlery from the cupboard and grab a couple sodas from the fridge. I place the sodas and cutlery on the small center table in front of Mitch. Feeling like a spare part in the kitchen, I ask Mitch for directions to the bathroom to freshen up for dinner. A small pile of clothes sits on top of the washer and a pile waiting to be folded in the dryer. I busy myself getting it sorted for Mitch. He needs to rest that shoulder and I have time before the food is ready.

Heading back to the kitchen, I watch the seconds tick on the clock. But my gaze doesn't stay on the clock for long. Instead, it finds Mitch and studies. The stubble on his face, the knife carved jawline, his pink lips. My gaze moves down to his thick bicep and his veiny hands placed on top of his large thigh muscle.

I gulp as I get lost in the desires inside my mind, if he gave in and stripped away this barrier in between us, would I stop him? If our work lives didn't matter and if I didn't have a stalker, would I give in and let him do with me as he pleases?

The oven ping yanks me back to the present, my mind slowly bringing itself back to now. Grabbing the oven mitts, I pull out the glass dish and place it on the side. God, it smells divine. Dishing up, I place a scoop onto both our plates and place the glass dish back into the oven before taking Mitch's plate over to him. He pats the empty space next to him, so I take a seat and put my plate on the table. Mitch hands me cutlery and a soda, and he goddamn winks at me before tucking in.

I spent three days with him and managed to control my mind, yet now I'm in a space that's purely Mitch, I'm losing my grip on myself.

I need to focus on something other than Mitch, so I put my mind to work. "I know I'm not supposed to ask," I swallow the soda in my mouth. "But how is the case going?"

"Tech finally got a pixelated photo of him. It's not perfect but it's enough. They'll get it cleaned up so we will know what he really looks like. We're keeping a close eye on the areas he's known to frequent. We're so close, Sas." He nods, his eyes sympathetic. "You'll get justice. I'll make sure of it."

"Just don't get shot... again." I tease him, placing a spoonful of food in my mouth.

"What, and not have you to nurse me back to health?" He recoils jokingly. "Any opportunity to have this ropa vieja again. This is unreal." He points at his food before licking his lips. "You're quite the chef, cereza."

"No." I shrug, waving him off. "It's a simple recipe from my abuela."

"Don't talk yourself down, Sas." He places his final spoonful in his mouth and puts his plate down. "This is *increíble*."

"Oh, please." I roll my eyes. "Stop talking me up. I'll never live up to a compliment like that." I laugh, lightly nudging him as I finish eating. "Do you need any help around here?" I ask, hoping he hasn't been cleaning up himself.

"It's okay. Jules has been helping me out after shifts." He checks his watch before picking up his phone and dialling a number. I don't want to eavesdrop, so I pick up our plates and take them to the sink.

"Hey." I turn around, but I notice Mitch is on the phone, so I focus on washing the dishes. "You don't need to stop by today, Saskia is here." I assume he's on the phone to Jules. He doesn't know she was the one who gave me his address. "See you later," he says as he ends the call.

"She's a good partner." I say, my hands scrubbing the remaining sauce off the plates.

"I won the lottery with her." Mitch confesses. I don't need to look at him to know he's smiling. "Her wife and kids are like my family."

"That's sweet." I smile at him over my shoulder. I'm glad he's not lonely and has people to turn to when he needs them.

I wash the few glasses in the bowl as Mitch stands next to me. He grabs the tea towel and begins drying the freshly washed dishes.

"You should be resting." I say sternly.

"I can dry some dishes, Sas." He shrugs, placing the plates in the cupboard.

"You shouldn't be reaching to put them away." I tell him, attempting to take them out of his grip, but he won't let me.

"I'm not reaching." He puts them above me. "You are."

He's not wrong. His extra eight inches on my height does mean he does less stretching. But I'm not having it.

"Sit down. I'm doing this." I frown, trying to take the tea towel from his grip.

"You sit down." He counters, trying to hide the smirk that's itching to make an appearance.

He won't let me have it, so I flick some cold water at him, unable to contain my chuckle, but I swallow it as soon as his gaze is pinned on me.

"Run." The words are thick with instruction, but I can see the playfulness swimming in his eyes.

I instinctively take a couple steps back around the breakfast bar, and he follows, but I can't get to the living area without him catching me, so I try to go the other way. A few steps back the way I came, but he mirrors me, still keeping me within arms reach.

I tell my legs to run, but my mind doesn't agree, so I stay still. "I don't want to run."

# 12

## SASKIA

My words are barely a whisper, but Mitch hears them.

He advances, his gaze set on me like I'm a meal and he hasn't eaten in days. Each one of his steps build desire thick in my stomach until the gap between us is nonexistent. I tilt my head up, his lips a few centimetres away from mine, his eyes glued on me.

He smells of sandalwood, mint and a hint of cherry, his breath steady but fast. My hands rest against his chest as his heart thrums in his chest, his hands slowly stroke down my back to my waist. His delicate touch leaves goosebumps assaulting my skin, desperate to feel his touch on my bare skin instead of over clothing.

His lips graze mine, the chance to taste him again is so close yet dangerous. But my mind doesn't focus on danger. It just focuses on *him*.

Just when I think he's going to give in, he lifts me onto the kitchen worktop, the hard material cool through my tights. He's flush against my skin, his crotch pressed against mine as his hand grips the back of my neck. His free hand loops around my waist, pulling me close, his lips skimming mine. And like a volcanic eruption, my stomach explodes as Mitch gives in. His lips crashing against mine, there isn't a single thought inside my mind. The only thing clouding my thoughts is Mitchell Alverez and how I'd do every single thing he'd ask of me, just to feel his mind controlling touch.

Rational thinking is out the window when it's just me, Mitch and the tension between us.

His tongue caresses and nudges the seam of mouth, asking for permission to enter. I gladly open for him, our mouths meld together like 2 parts of the same coin. He dominates my mouth, hot and wet, as I struggle to catch my breath. His lips are my lifeline and I can't let go, yet each taste of him is only making me weaker.

His grip on my ass is strong as he carries me to the bedroom without a struggle. I'm careful not to touch near his stitches, but before I can tighten my arms around his neck, he drops me back onto his bed. It's soft and inviting as his cotton duvet does nothing to soothe the heat radiating from my body.

Mitch is standing over me, his muscles visible through his thin clothes and his erect cock straining against his joggers. It's only an outline, but it's big.

My pussy dampens at the sight.

He strips off my boots and grasps the waistband of my tights, yanking them in one pull, my panties going with them.

I can't stop the yelp from leaving my lips.

Mitch wastes no time pulling my dress over my head, my breasts bouncing free. "Fuck." He growls, his eyes drinking me in like I'm his favorite cocktail.

I'm growing impatient as my need to see him bare in front of me becomes overwhelming. I sit up, my eyes focused on him as I lift the hem of his shirt. He smirks, reaching his hand behind his head and pulling the fabric over his head. He discards it on the floor, along with my clothes. The waistband of his joggers are an invitation to see what's below as my hands snake underneath and begin pulling down. Each painful inch after inch, his cock springs free, and I almost choke on my own saliva. Eight inches and thick, I consider making an escape plan before I end up in pain. But my pussy doesn't let me.

"Come here." Mitch's smirk is devilish as he holds two hands out.

I hold them as he pulls me to my feet. He spins behind me and sits on the bed, tapping his lap and grabbing my hips as he lowers me to sit in front of him. My back is flush against his warm chest as his dick is trapped underneath me, his length pressed against every part of my core. I can't resist moving my hips because it feels so good.

"If you keep moving like that, this will be over before it's begun, and we can't have that." Mitch whispers in my ear as his hands clamp around my hips, halting my movement. "That's what you do to me." His lips graze my neck as he inhales my scent. "That's how much I want you, cereza."

Lifting my chin, I meet Mitch's eyes in the full length mirror in front of us. His gaze makes my legs weak, his irises swimming with desire as he studies my body.

"Tell me if you want me to stop," he hums against my ear, his palms in between my legs, slowly pulling them apart.

"I trust you." I say, the cool air kissing my pussy.

He nods like my words satisfy him. "We need a safe word." His sternness is still sexy as dominance drips from his tone. "You say it and I'll stop, okay?"

I nod, my eyes flicking to the right while I think of a word. "Cherry." I smirk. It's my favorite fruit and I wear my cherry necklace every day without fail. It's a perfect choice.

I don't miss his chuckle as he nods.

My pussy is exposed as Mitch places his head on my right shoulder, my legs are hooked over his thighs and pulled open wide, my back against his warm chest. He places both my hands on the outside of his toned thighs as he slowly touches along mine. Each second feels like an overwhelming edge as he teases me. He's a few inches from my core, yet he's not touching. The tension vibrates inside of me.

My eyes fall shut as a moan slips past my lips, my body humming in response. I try to calm my fast breathing, but his right hand snakes across my thigh and skims my pussy making my breath catch. His finger finds my clit, rubbing gentle circles as his left hand finds my breast. He pinches my nipple gently, the buzzing feeling shooting straight between my thighs. "Look at yourself." He tells me, my eyes meeting my own flustered expression in the mirror. I'd rather look at him, but I do as I'm told. "Look at how beautiful you are. Every inch of you is made to perfection."

"Mitch." I moan, barely able to get my words out. I don't know what I'm trying to say as my eyes fall closed from the bliss happening between my legs. I feel like I'm under a magnifying glass, but I want him to study every inch of me. To peel back the layers and see who I really am.

But then he stops his movements. My eyes fall back on his in the mirror, mischief swimming in his irises. "Keep watching, else I'll stop."

I moan in protest, but I gaze back at the mirror, watching his finger circling my clit.

"That's a good girl." He praises me, and I nearly melt in his arms. His left hand leaves my nipple, and I'm about to put it back onto it, but his hand snakes under my ass and finds my entrance. Circling teasingly, I whimper for his touch. Slowly, he pumps his middle finger inside of my pussy at a constant pace, still circling my clit in unison.

I'm panting, my eyes still on the mirror as sweat gathers on my forehead. I can barely comprehend the man inviting me to reach my high. He was just a detective on my case one day, and now he's got me spread in front of a mirror as he finger fucks me.

Adding another finger, I moan in approval as my pussy feels full. I can't stop myself from thrusting into his touch as he picks up his pace and circles my clit with more pressure. I can feel his dick throbbing with need, the erotic touch only making me more desperate to taste him.

Each move he makes builds more pressure inside of me as my orgasm builds, my breathing becoming erratic and desperate. "I'm going to cum, Mitch." The words are delirium from my lips. My hands snake into the bed sheet as I climb a ladder of pleasure.

"Good girl. Cum for me, cereza." He coos, his hot breath on my ear sending shivers down my spine.

I do as I'm told and clench around his fingers, his name falling from my lips as I come. My back arches as my eyes struggle to focus on my panting figure, white dots assaulting my vision. My ears thrum as ecstasy pulls me higher, my body feeling weightless and full of pleasure.

I can barely catch my breath as I come down from my orgasm. I think my body is calming down, but Mitch withdraws his fingers, his eyes pinned on me in the mirror, and he pulls his soaked fingers to his mouth, licking off every drop of my juices. His eyes close as he moans his satisfaction, and I nearly come from the sight alone.

"Perfection." He drinks me in, his cock warm against my back.

Barely able to stand on my wobbling legs, I rise and turn around to face Mitch, dropping to my knees in front of him.

"This was about you." He hums as he leans backwards, a playful smile on his face. It's hard to compare the man I know as Detective Alvarez with this sinful God laying in front of me. Running my palms along his thick thighs, his muscles rippling beneath as his 8-pack tenses.

"And this is what I want." I respond, taking his cock in my hand. Pumping a few times, I size him up with my eyes before placing his tip in my mouth. A drop of precum hits my taste buds, salty yet sweet. I bob up and down, slowly introducing more length as I move my hand in time with my movements.

"Fuck, Sas." He groans, his head falling back as his fingers lace through my hair. His grip is strong yet encouraging. "Tan jodidamente perfecto". His words are strained as his free hand clenches the bedsheet.

*So fucking perfect.*

Words in our native tongue are so fucking sexy.

Looking up at him through my lashes, I stop sucking, just to see his reaction. His head shoots up in protest as his eyebrows dip. "Watch yourself." I instruct, catching my own smirk on my face as I turn to the mirror, showing him where to look. "Else I'll stop."

"Fair play, cereza." He hums, nodding with that devilish smile on his face that drives me crazy.

Focusing on his own reflection, he grips my hair with both hands. I wrap my lips around his cock and begin sucking, this time faster and deeper. His tip hits the back of my throat repeatedly, my gag reflex trying to make an appearance, but I force it away. I welcome his length with each suck, as he guides my head with his hands. My eyes water as fat tears fall down my cheeks, and I can't stop myself from looking up at him. A clenched jaw, hooded eyes and a thick pool of desire swimming in his brown eyes.

His thighs begin clenching as his mouth falls open, his groans becoming erratic. "Fuck Sas, I'm going to cum." His voice is weak as his hands grip harder.

I welcome the sting on my scalp as I begin sucking faster, my hands at his base for extra grip. My jaw aches in the best way as Mitch moans my name on repeat like he's chanting his favorite song. And it so happens to be my favorite, too.

Thick ropes of cum hit the back of my throat, but I keep sucking. I suck him through his orgasm as his body shakes and his muscles contract, not stopping until he slows his moans.

With a loud pop, I lick off any extra juice from his cock, unable to resist the taste of him.

"Open." He commands, removing his hands from my hair to place them on my jaw. He lifts my head to look at him, and I do as I say. My tongue darts out to show him the pretty picture he painted inside of my mouth as his eyes swim with darkness.

Possession.

"Swallow." His words are stern and I obey. "Good girl."

The warm liquid is down my throat in one gulp, but I want more. I need more of him.

"Please." I beg as he picks me up, my legs wrapping around his waist.

"Please what, cereza?" He acts oblivious as he lowers me down onto his mattress and climbs on top of me.

"Fuck me, Mitch." My words are thick with need as I look up at him. I don't miss his look of pride as his hands explore my body. "I'm clean."

"I know, baby." His lips leave soft kisses down my neck. "So am I." Each kiss leaves a burning path of need in it's wake, and I'm so fucking desperate to have him inside of me. The thought of having anything in between is too much. Normally I insist on a condom, but not this time.

His mouth latches onto my left breast as he sucks and bites, forcing a gasp from my lips, but he soothes it with a warm kiss straight afterwards. Paying my right breast the same amount of attention, he licks up my chest, all the way to my lips.

His mouth hovers over my ear, his hot breath leaving goosebumps along my skin. "I think about you all the time, Sas." His confession feels like a blossom of satisfaction in my stomach as butterflies consume me. "I can't tell you how many times I've touched myself to the thought of you." A gentle nibble on my ear. "I think about how well you'd take my cock." He kisses along my jawline. "How loud you'd moan when I fuck you." His mouth hovers above my lips as his eyes look deep into mine. "How defeated you look when you cum."

I swear I nearly melt into the mattress. I feel desired. Wanted. Needed. My core heats with need at the thought of him experiencing his desires in real life. I want to give him that. I want to give myself that experience.

"Please." I whimper, my hands snaking along his back as I try to pull his body closer.

Like two magnets, his lips crash against mine as he takes all he needs from me.

His cock teases my entrance and in a slow motion, he pushes inside of me one inch at a time. We gasp in unison as I adjust to his size. My eyes fall onto his cock entering me before I let out a moan.

"I'll take it slow, baby." He kisses my forehead, before looping his hand around my back to hold my hips up slightly.

I nod as my teeth nibble on my bottom lip, my nails gripping into his skin as he thrusts. The movement feels goddamn perfect as I adjust to his size. Each thrust is an edge closer to the orgasm building low in my belly but I try to push it away. I want this to last forever. I've had him inside of me for barely twenty seconds, yet I'm already addicted to the feeling he creates inside of me.

Mitch picks up his pace as he bottoms out his pelvis hitting my clit at the perfect angle and my breasts bounce with each thrust, whimpers fall from my lips as he hits that sensitive spot deep inside of me.

My eyes fall to his stitches as I remember his no strenuous activity rule. "What about your wound?" I frown through each pant.

"I can handle it." He coos, placing a kiss on my lips before looping both arms under my thighs. I interlock my hands behind his head as he walks us into the living room, my pussy full of his throbbing cock.

Our lips are touching but we don't kiss. Instead, he stands in the middle of the room and slowly moves my ass back and forwards, fucking me standing up.

Sweat gathers on both our foreheads as our bodies mould together perfectly. Moans and gasps fall from my lips as I feel him so deeply inside of me. My body feels full of bliss; this is the type of sex people dream of. This is the kind of sex I fantasized about when I made myself cum thinking of Mitch.

I can't stop my head from falling backwards as he picks up his pace. My breasts rub against his skin as my nipples tingle from the constant stimulation. God, this feels like a drug has taken control of my body and keeps me on top of my highest high.

I attempt to kiss him, but I can't stop the moans from leaving my mouth as Mitch groans in response.

"You're taking me so fucking well, cereza." His words are breathless as he fucks me hard. "I'm never letting you go, Sas. You're mine." I can't find my words, so I nod. I nod so much because I don't want him to let me go. "You're fucking made for me."

He walks us backwards to the couch and lowers us down but keeps his cock buried deep inside of me as I straddle him. I can feel my orgasm building, so I use his shoulders for stability and begin bouncing. Mitch grabs my hips and helps me out as he lifts me up and down harder, looking down between us as my pussy swallows him whole.

Each thrust is a push closer to my high as my legs begin shaking and my arms feel weak. "I'm going to cum, Mitch." I whine, my heartbeat nearly pounding out of my chest.

"Fuck, so am I, baby." He growls, his grip on my hips tightening.

An explosion of euphoria engulfs me as my orgasm pushes itself to its peak. My vision is blurred as my body feels weightless. My pussy convulses as his cock throbs inside of me, emptying himself as he rides us through our high. Lust takes over both of us as we whimper into each other's mouths, our bodies gravitating towards each other. My body floats on a cloud of pure bliss as each nerve ending inside of me has been awoken and simultaneously calmed.

I struggle to catch my breath as I slow my bouncing and Mitch slows his thrusts as he gently caresses the top of my thighs.

*That was mind blowing.*

I can't take my eyes off of him as I drink him in. He's flustered and out of breath, but he never takes his eyes off of me. His hands slowly stroke up my arms and my neck before he stops on my cheeks, as he sits himself up slightly and places a gentle kiss on my lips. Not full of passion this time. It's reassuring and tender. Like he's savoring every moment between us.

And for a moment, I forgot the hell that's going on in my life. I felt safe with him before but this is another level. He provides me with a safe space that I revel in. A place I never want to leave, because I don't feel the need to check over my shoulder when I'm with Mitch. He's safety and security, but he's also soothing and compassionate.

"Let's get you cleaned up." He smiles, scooping me up in his arms before carrying me to the bathroom.

He turns on the shower and checks the temperature before carrying me in and stepping under the water with me. He washes me with a softness that I want to bottle up to keep forever, before drying me and taking me to bed.

He's tired me out in the best way, and now I have him in my corner, I don't think I can go a single day without him.

Sometimes, the things in life that are meant for you, sit right in front of your eyes and only make themselves visible when you're ready for them.

# 13

# MITCHELL

I thought I'd be waking up with a sore shoulder, but instead, I'm blooming with satisfaction. My muscles ache in the best way and my heart feels full of happiness.

I gave in last night. This isn't something I should be giving into, but it's not something I regret, either. In fact, we're closer than we've ever been; she stuck by me at the hospital, even if that was my doing, and it feels like we've gotten to know each other more than just colleagues or work relationships.

She's my first thought in the morning and my last thought at night, and the woman who takes over my dreams. We've built a friendship between us, but friends shouldn't want to fuck each other the way I want her. Having her bare and ready for me;

each inch of her skin on display so I can study her and please every raw centimeter of her is a fucking dream come true.

Seeing Saskia with her legs spread in the mirror, doing as I asked, was mind blowing, but watching every inch of my cock slowly disappear inside my perfect pussy was unreal. She's a drug I'm addicted to. There's no fucking way I'll be listening to anyone who tells me I shouldn't be with her. I can't let her go now that I have her.

I woke up before Saskia this morning and I could barely pull myself out of bed. I wanted to stay next to her, my arms wrapped around her perfect skin, inhaling her addictive cherry scent. Last night keeps replaying in my mind like a film that I never want to end. Every second of it was perfect. I'd spent hours imagining Saskia in all those vulnerable ways, but it wasn't how I thought it would be. It was intoxicating. Each second was electrifying and breathtaking. She's faultless; created by the gods without a single imperfection.

Carrying a cup of coffee and a bottle of water, I enter my bedroom as I bring Saskia what she needs to hydrate. Her eyes dart over to me, heavy but awake. "Good morning, pretty girl." I coo, placing the drinks down on the bedside table. "Sleep well?"

A smile instantly pulls at her cheeks. "Best night sleep I've had in a while," she nods.

I kiss her on the forehead as she looks up at me with those beautiful brown eyes. God, I'm addicted to her. I need her close; to touch and taste her. Revel in her essence until I die.

"Let's start your morning off the same way." I affirm, my hands finding the cover and pulling it down slowly, exposing her bare body. My eyes roam over the pure perfection in front of me as I memorize each inch of her body.

She smiles as mischief swims in her eyes, looking down at me expectantly.

I drop my head, my lips grazing along her delicate neck. The light touch makes her shiver as goosebumps attack her skin. I place soft kisses around her perfect tits as her nipples pebble in response, down her stomach and on her thighs before pausing exactly where I need to be. Grasping my hands on the inside of her thighs, I pry them open and pull her closer to me. Her pussy is wet and hot, and I have to fight the urge not to cum right then.

I kiss down her pubic bone but hover above her core as I gaze up at her. She's flustered but needy as she nibbles her lip. Lowering my head, I grip her ass and dart my tongue out, tasting her, licking her from her entrance to her clit. I can't stop the lengthy moan that leaves my lips as I vibrate against her folds.

Saskia's hands find my hair as she yanks and soothes with strokes.

I begin slowly licking and sucking her folds, making sure to pay attention to every part of her pretty pink pussy, apart from where she wants it most. She squirms and pulls my head, so I lock my arms around the back of her thighs and hold her still.

"I'll get there when I'm good and ready. Now, lay back and enjoy, because I intend to." I don't hear what she says as her legs tighten around my head and I get lost in her pussy. I lap her up before gently circling her clit with the tip of my tongue, her body clenches and vibrates. I can't help the smile on my face as I suck her clit between my lips and alternate between flicking and licking.

My satisfaction hums out loud as I admire her perfect pussy. She grinds against my tongue, which only encourages me to feast on the perfect meal in front of me. "You taste like heaven." The words fall from my lips as I lap up her delicious juices. "And you taste like mine."

Her head falls back and her mouth falls open as she moans and pants my name like she's part of a goddamn cult. It awakens a primal desire inside of me as she says my name. My cock strains against my joggers, but I refuse to touch it. This is about Saskia and how fucking much I need to taste her.

My tongue fucks her entrance as her back arches and she cries out unabashed. She's warm and addictive, her pussy was made for me and me only. Her grip on my hair stings as she lets her fingers get lost in my strands, but the harmless pain only makes me eat her more intensely.

Moving back up to her clit, I pay special attention as I grip her thighs, eating her with no mercy. I'm fucking starving and Saskia is the only meal on my menu.

Sliding two fingers inside her wet pussy, I begin finger fucking her as I suck her clit. I move my tongue and fingers in unison as I soak up her blushed state. There's not a single artist in this world that could paint a picture as perfect as Saskia Hernandez.

Her panting and moans become louder as she hums, nodding as I pick up my pace. "Fuck, Mitch. This is so much better than I imagined." She cries, her forehead glistening with sweat beads.

I can't help but smirk as I look up at her. "Imagined?" I question between licks.

"You're not the only one who touched themselves at the thought." She raises her eyebrows seductively before a whimper leaves her lips. "Thinking of you made me cum so hard that my legs were shaking."

"Fuck, Sas." Hot liquid spills inside my joggers at the thought of Saskia touching herself to the thought of me. She's made me fucking come in my own pants like a teenager. She has so much control over me that I'd break my own legs if she asked.

I devour her like I'm a staved man, not a single inch of her delectable pussy left untouched. Her juices are dripping down my fingers as her pussy begins clenching around them, so I flick her clit with more pressure.

"I'm coming, Mitch!" She cries, one hand finding her nipple as she rubs, while her other hand is pushing my head down.

Her pussy milks my fingers as she screams her ecstasy out loud, grinding against my face and arching her back. My name is falling from her lips like a perfect hymn, I can't take my eyes off of her.

I keep going until she's ridden out her orgasm, then I slowly withdraw my fingers and place them into my mouth. My eyes roll to the back of my head as I savor every drop of her come, memorizing it on my tastebuds until I can get my next fix.

Saskia's flustered state is a mental image I save.

I need to get us both cleaned up, but first, I need her in my arms. Laying next to her and pulling her close, I kiss her swollen lips. "Can I pick you up after work and we'll go out to dinner?" I ask, my nose nuzzled into her tight curls.

"Are you allowed?" She asks, turning her head to face me.

"Of course, cereza." I smile. "I'll grab you at seven." I sit up, trying to find the energy to get myself off the bed to clean us up, but Saskia's hand grabs mine and pulls me back down. "Come on," I nod, attempting my best stern face.

"Damn." She rolls her eyes as her cheeks lift. "Why do people have to commit crimes?" She shrugs at the inconvenience.

I can't stop the chuckle from leaving my mouth. "I have no idea, baby. If they didn't though, we'd both be out of a job."

She nods. "That's true. I'm just bitter that I can't spend the day with you." She cuddles into me and I pull her closer so she's flush against my chest.

"Me too, baby." I laugh, rubbing soft circles on her cheeks.

I've made my decision and I don't give a fuck if it costs my job. I want Saskia Hernandez, and now that I have her, I'm not letting go.

The past twenty-four hours have been unreal, I've never felt better. We haven't discussed what we are and what is going on between us, but I don't feel the need to discuss it right this second. After last night, letting her go feels like losing a part of me. It's just not going to fucking happen.

I showered her, got her dressed and dropped her home to get herself ready for work. There's no cops outside her house after I informed them she wouldn't be returning home yesterday, so they put their efforts elsewhere. Once she got herself ready, I dropped her at work and made my way to the police station.

I'm greeted with smiles and handshakes, with well wishes and welcome backs. I've not even been off work for a week, yet people are acting like I've been away for a month. I feel wanted here. It's a great feeling to return to.

I head towards my desk instinctively, my eyes darting around for my team, but none of them are here. There should be at least one of them on the floor, but I'm met with colleagues who are lower rank. Frowning, I pull out my phone to see if I have any messages, but my phone doesn't have a single notification. I know I've returned to work a few days earlier than planned, but I didn't tell anyone, so nothing should be out of the ordinary.

Something isn't right.

Unease grabs me by the throat and pulls me under as I try to make sense of what's happening. I notice Captain Wallace's office door is shut, so I walk over and lightly rap my knuckles against the glass.

"Come in!" His words sound defeated, even through a pane of glass.

Opening the wooden door, I'm met with my whole team staring back at me. Jules, Cap, Sergeant Fields, Hackett and Marten all glare at me, before averting their gaze over to Cap.

"You shouldn't be back yet." Captain Wallace's tone is firm as he rubs his bald head.

I frown, taken aback by the unwelcoming welcome back from my team. "Well, I am. My shoulder's fine. I'm losing the will to live in my apartment." I state, closing the door behind me. "What's going on?"

"This isn't the welcome back you deserve, Alvarez." Sergeant Fields begins, crossing his arms over his chest. "But something important has come up."

I stare at him, waiting for him to continue, but he doesn't. Instead, he looks at Jules silently, communicating something to her through his eyes.

"Someone tell me what's going on before I lose my shit." I grunt, trying to keep my voice at a normal decibel, but agitation is burning my veins.

"We were sent this." Jules holds out an A5, sand colored envelope, which is opened at the top by a letter opener. I grab some evidence gloves from behind me and slide them onto my hands, before taking the envelope off Jules' hands. Pulling out the single piece of card, my eyes focus in on the photo that's been taken and printed out.

Rage. Pure burning rage ignites every neuron inside my body. I feel pure hatred towards the person who took this photo. I feel violated. Devastated. Resentment. But mostly, I feel an overpowering sense of protection over Saskia. Knowing how much this will break her is destroying me. I know she won't recover from this. The small steps she's taken these past couple weeks to overcome her anxiety is going to be shattered, along with her heart.

I'm going to have to tell her.

I'm going to have to show her.

Bile threatens to leave my stomach just as realization washes over me.

I'm going to have to live with the fact I've brought this on. If I used my goddamn self restraint and didn't get involved with

Saskia, I wouldn't have made her a target again. I've practically stuck the red target on her bare body, for her stalker to mark.

I'm going to fucking strangle him when I get him.

No one violates my girl and lives to tell the tale.

My hands may be clean right now, but sooner or later, they'll be soaking in the blood of Saskia's stalker. Each drop he leaves is a shed of sorrow he should be sending Saskia's way. I won't stop until he absolves his sins.

# 14

## SASKIA

I think my good luck is still going, because the urgent call from Captain Wallace can only mean one thing. They've caught Chris and today is the day I get closure.

Practically running over to the police station, I ignore the sting in my ankles as my high heels remind me they aren't suitable running shoes. My feet burn with each step I take up the stairs to the main doors, but I ignore it. I'm too focused on making it upstairs to Captain Wallace's office so I can finally have peace of mind.

His office door is shut, so I lightly knock, listening for a go ahead to enter, but one never comes. Instead, I can hear

Mitch inside, shouting, so I push the handle down and open the door.

Like I've made a sudden loud noise, Mitch and his whole team turns to face me, with sympathy marked on their faces. My good luck suddenly feels like a distant dream as dread sets deep in my stomach. I want to know what's wrong, but I'm too afraid to ask, because I know the second I do, my world will shatter around me.

I step in the office, slowly closing the door behind me. Mitch has his head in his hand, inhaling slowly, and the sight of him being uneasy just elicits a whole new level of worry inside of me. He's always the strong one. The one who holds me together and keeps me safe. If something has him this rattled, it's not good.

"Miss Hernandez," Captain Wallace clears his throat, rising to his full height.

"Saskia, please." I interrupt, the lump in my throat forcing me to swallow.

"Saskia," he starts again, lowering his shoulders. "We need to prepare you for what you're about to see."

"Okay." My pitch is higher and barely audible as my heartbeat feels erratic inside of my chest. Not only is Mitch's team acting weird, but I swear I'm about to have a heart attack from the debilitating anticipation.

"It's going to make you feel belittled, embarrassed." Jules speaks, her eyes soft and full of sorrow. "But we're right here for you. Okay?"

I really don't like where this is going. My blood is pumping inside of me, the feeling making me lightheaded.

"Please, just tell me." The words are a light whisper from my lips. My voice feels obliterated, just like any positive feeling inside of me.

Stepping towards me, he places a hand behind my back and rubs soothing circles as Jules hands me some blue rubber gloves. I assume they're to put on, so I slide them onto my hands, struggling to stop them from shaking. Jules then hands me a large envelope that's been cut open at the top. Peeking inside, I see one piece of card with a yellow post-it note stuck to it. Unsticking the post-it note and pulling it out, I read the scribbled handwriting.

*Is this what Casamount's finest does to victims?*

I recoil as a frown takes over my face. It doesn't make any sense, so I put the post-it note on top of the envelope and pull out the card. I can't figure it out at first, so I carry on pulling until it's almost fully out. My eyes glance upwards, taking in the expressions of Mitch's team, trying to ignore the sickening feeling deep in my gut.

Placing the card on top of the envelope, I glance down, curious to find out what has this team so on edge.

My heart stops beating in my chest.

I see what has them so devastated, because the second my eyes meet the photo the police department was sent, I swear I feel my heart crack.

And it carries on cracking the more I look at the photo. One crack after the other, shooting pains explode in my chest as I struggle to contain the tears gathering on my lash line.

A photo taken of me and Mitch, both naked and having sex in his apartment. He's holding me up by my thighs as my arms are wrapped around his neck, in his living room. Someone across the way took the photo, blew it up and sent it to the police department like some sick, twisted game.

This isn't a game. This is my life. It's Mitch's life. It's his career.

I'm going to throw up, but I swallow down the burning bile threatening to make an appearance.

"Who's seen this?" I ask, the words barely leaving my mouth.

"Only the people in this room." Captain Wallace says, his features turned down as he looks at me with sorrow.

I feel violated. Like everything about me never has a safety net to protect private things in my life. I know it's not the team's fault they've seen this, and I'm somewhat grateful it's only been seen by those in this room, but it doesn't stop me from feeling exposed.

"What's going to happen to Mitch?" I ask him, hot tears falling down my cheeks. If he loses his career because some sick stalker finds joy in ruining lives, I'll never forgive myself.

"Don't worry about me, Sas." Mitch says against my head, but his words aren't convincing. I can hear the worry in his voice.

"I do." The words leave my mouth without thinking. "It's not fair on you."

"Well," Sergeant Fields sighs. "There are certain factors that would change the outcome of this situation."

"And what would they be?" Mitch questions, his hand still planted firmly on my back. I feel his reassurance through his touch.

"When the relationship started, how close the victim is to the case, how this would affect the case outcome." Sergeant

Fields props himself on the corner of a desk with his hands interlocked.

"I'll recuse myself if I have to." Mitch shrugs. "I don't want to, but if it means Saskia will get justice, then I will."

Guilt turns my stomach to ice. I'm starting to think whether justice is even worth it. But I deserve justice. Any woman who has been stalked, violated and belittled deserves justice.

"Let's not make any decisions yet." Captain Wallace puts his hand up to stop Mitch. "There's a misleading factor here and it's our conversation we had at the courthouse the day Saskia got arrested."

*Like I needed that reminder.*

"Cap, I knew what the conversation meant. There's a difference between protecting a victim of a case and sleeping with one." Mitch's response burns, but it's true. His tightened grip is a sign of reassurance and I soak in every second of it.

"But that's not where this started." Jules takes a couple steps towards Mitch. "You've known Saskia for over a year, since before this case." She throws her hands up. "I mean, you were crushing on her for ages before you even spoke to her." Jules talks out of the side of her mouth like she just told some major secret, and the way Mitch sighs, tells me it was something they kept between them.

*Damn.* The butterflies in my stomach are on an adrenaline rush the way they're fluttering.

"You're colleagues. Maybe not in the same way as we are," she flicks her index finger between her and Mitch. "But you both work for the justice system." She shrugs nonchalantly.

"I never viewed her as a victim." Mitch misses the point of Jules' statement, and runs to defend me instead. I can't ignore the warmness enveloping me.

"That's not what she's saying." My voice is croaky, and I cough slightly to clear my throat. "We knew each other before the case, so there's no way this can be spun into a story of you stepping over the line or taking advantage of me."

"I won't allow a defence lawyer to ruin this case for the sake of their reputation." Captain Wallace squares his shoulders as he crosses his arms. "Someone get that envelope to the lab for fingerprints testing."

My gut sinks. More people gawking at the evidence that is a private moment between me and Mitch. A moment that shouldn't have been witnessed by anyone else, let alone Mitch's colleagues.

I can't be here anymore. I need fresh air and silence. A place I can be alone to process what's just happened. I thought he left me alone. Lost interest in me when he saw the police presence and Mitch around keeping me safe. But instead of backing off, he's taken it a step further and violated me. *With* police protection.

God, this is demoralizing.

"I have to go back to work." My voice is still hushed, but it comes out loud enough for Mitch to hear.

"Let me drop you." He opens the office door and waits for me to follow his lead.

I leave the room, not having the energy to say goodbye to everyone. Honestly, I can barely look them in the eye. "It's okay, Mitch. The courtroom is literally across the street. I can walk." I walk backwards toward the door as he grips my hand.

His eyes plead with me as he steps in my direction. "You don't need to walk, Sas." I can barely refuse his request. But I need to.

"But I want to walk, Mitch. Please. I need the fresh air." I squeeze his hand for reassurance. He's overprotective; I understand that. But he also needs to trust me. Just because I have a stalker, doesn't mean I should lose myself, besides, with the amount of law enforcement, I doubt he'd make a move.

I can see the internal battle going on behind his eyes as he looks away from me, but after a short amount of time, he sighs and turns his attention to me. "It's not safe." His hand softly trails down my arm.

"It's a very public walk in the middle of the day. I'm as cautious as the next guy, but he's not that stupid." I try to reassure him, but if I'm honest, I'm not even sure I believe my own words. I'm scared of the man who drugged and kidnapped me, and I know that fear won't go until he's locked up, but anyone with half a brain would plan their kidnapping tactics to a time where there aren't witnesses.

"Fine." He shakes his head. "But I'm walking you out." He points his finger at me with raised eyebrows, his expression telling me not to question it.

A small laugh slips past my lips. Leading the way, I make my way down the stairs and past reception, with Mitch hot on my trail. He keeps a hand on my lower back as he guides me out the door. I've grown used to having him close by as my protector. It's a security blanket for me, knowing any danger that could possibly face me would be batted away by Mitch. I'm thankful for it, but I worry about his own safety. You can only look danger in the face so many times until it drags you down with it.

Casamount's cool air hits me as I exit the police station. Pulling my beige duster coat together, I try my best to ward off the chill.

"I'll see you later?" I turn on my heel, peering up at Mitch.

I can still see the unhappy look in his eyes, but he's always given me my freedom. "I'll pick you up at seven." His large hand cups my cheeks as he places a warm kiss on my lips. It's dominating, and it momentarily makes me forget everything that's happening at the moment.

"See you at seven." I hum, smiling as I walk away from the station.

I cross the road and turn around to see Mitch still standing outside, watching me. I try to focus on walking one foot in front of the other, but knowing he's watching me makes me feel giddy. Like he has the power to forget everything terrible in my life, I almost forgot what happened half an hour ago. There's no certainty that the photo is from Chris, but my gut is telling me it was. He's playing with me, toying with me. But this time, I'm not enough. He's toying with the police department, too, not caring for the consequences. Men who don't consider the ramifications of their actions are dangerous. Deadly. Predators that are a threat to humanity.

That's exactly what Chris is.

I take another peek behind me as I cross the halfway point, just before I head down a short alleyway, and I can no longer see Mitch's outline. The realization that I'm truly alone now hits me. No one to defend and protect me. Just me, with no defence mechanism and the instinct to recoil from danger.

Maybe I should have let Mitch take me. But I needed time to think. Time to really *think* about that photo, the consequences and the threat looming over me.

Things with Mitch aren't simple. They feel like they are when it's just us, but it's not always going to be that way. Our jobs can be time consuming; the constant worry of someone using our relationship over him makes me feel guilty.

But some things are worth fighting for. Mitch certainly is. I'm sure of it...but guilt snakes it's tight hands around my back.

Except it's not guilt wrapping its hands around me, it's a dooming feeling, warning me that danger is mere feet away from me. My body tries to freeze, but I force my legs to keep walking forward. I don't allow myself to turn around or investigate what this feeling is, I just pace forward.

But my pace isn't getting me away from danger.

Because my brain signals are no longer working.

A cloth is suddenly placed over my nose and mouth, suffocating me from oxygen. A switch is flipped inside of me, firing up every ounce of strength I have to run, scream, fight back, do anything, but it's not enough.

It's never enough.

What I assume is chloroform takes over me quicker than I can refuse, and my surroundings dull. The end of the alleyway is so close, but my legs won't work and I suddenly feel invisible.

Tears warm my cheeks as my consciousness finally dips.

"Let's finish what I started, shall we?"

The voice is a reminder of the worst night of my life as defeat drowns me.

*Chris.*

# 15

## SASKIA

My mind is foggy and my head feels like it's splitting in half, the constant throbbing is intense. My thoughts feel disordered; nothing makes sense. I try to remember the last thing I did, but all I can remember is being at the police station. I'm not sure why I was there, though.

My eyes sting as I try to open them slightly, but the lack of lighting in this place is making it near impossible to see anything. I can see a small square in the corner, with boards placed over it. It looks like a window by the way the light is slicing through the small gaps. Those small rays magnify the dust in the air. Hundreds of speckles float in the line of light, making me realize how many more are lurking in the darkness.

This room smells musty, with a tinge of charcoal marinating in the air. I'm not sure if there's a fireplace in here, but if there's not, then I'm worried. Charcoal is known for absorbing the smell of death, and I'm starting to realize it may be for me.

I try to pull my hand to my head to soften the pounding, but I can't move it. Yanking, I make no leeway in freeing my hands as panic claws up my throat. I try my legs, but they're bound together so tightly that I can't even attempt to stand.

My brain filters to survival mode as I try to make sense of what's happening. But my mind is a blank space and there's no reminder to bring back those memories. How can I piece together the past when I only have half the puzzle?

I need to think of a way to get out of here, some way of getting out of these duct tape restraints.

But instead, my body freezes. Loud, heavy-footed steps are moving above me. Laying quietly, I try to listen for other people, but so far there's only one person who would want me as their puppet. They're calm, calculated, and authoritative. Like the person is in control of the situation and not panicking they've taken someone hostage.

A loud squeak pulls me from my dreaded thoughts as a light shines down some rotted, wooden stairs. I'm able to glance around and see where I am, but there's not much in this room.

It's a basement of some sort, with red carpets and walls covered in ripped wallpaper. It was blue, I think, but the majority is gone, with stained plaster left in its place.

Glancing around for anything I can use, I'm left with nothing but defeat as the only thing I see is chains that attach me to a wall and the dirty, white mattresses below me with shadows of objects in the corner.

I gulp, the next steps flashing in front of my eyes like an assaulting camera flash. I'm defenceless, with no one to help me and no weapon to defend myself.

*And there's no fireplace.*

Heavy footsteps start descending the stairs, and it feels like I'm being sucked into a lion's den. Weak, useless and restrained, I sit here for that animal to do with me as he pleases. Can I even put up a fight? The second I try, I'll probably be knocked out again. And I don't like not knowing what's happening to me. Unconsciousness isn't an option.

The door above suddenly slams and a yelp leaves my mouth as I try to hold back my tears. The terror is overwhelming, but I grab at every ounce of control I have inside of me and attempt to compose myself. I have to survive this, he will not break me.

But composure doesn't last long when a small bulb light flicks on above my head, and Chris looms over me like a demon during sleep paralysis. He's grinning, but there's no humor in it. It's intimidating and horrifying, as his wide eyes gawk at me with purpose. "Missed me, sweetheart?" His coffee breath fans across my face, the smell putrid and overpowering.

Recollection comes flooding through my brain as my memory loss is restored. I was at the station for that goddamn photo. Mitch walked me out. I wouldn't let him walk me back to court. How stupid am I? And then it hits me.

*Mitch.*

After all he's done to keep me safe, I go and fuck it up.

I can't find words as my mouth falls open. Instead, fat tears roll down my cheek and onto my trousers.

"I missed you." His swollen finger swipes down my cheek, gathering a stray tear. He looks at it like it's an insect found in the garden. He lifts it to his lips and swipes his tongue out to taste it. I fight my body to not recoil, but when he hums in satisfaction, nausea threatens to make an appearance. "I've been keeping an eye on you." He shrugs like it's not a big deal, when it's nearly ruined my life. "That bartender at the Rose Cavern had to snitch when he saw me doing a good deed, carrying the drunk girl out the bar." Rolling his eyes, he rises to his feet and walks back and forth. "I'm not finished with him.

He'll pay for ruining my plan, but luckily for me, I've got you back." His eyes lift as he smiles.

I shake my head, the tears slowing. "Please let me go." I say as my voice shakes, but the second the words leave my lips, I regret it. My denial is his satisfaction.

"No." He says so plainly like it was a passing question. "I have a question for you." Pointing his index finger at me, he stops pacing to look at me and crouches down to my sitting height. "Did you like the picture?" Pinning me with a glare, his smile is full of animosity.

I can't hide my hatred as my eyes scowl back at him as I bite my tongue. I don't want to give him the satisfaction, so I don't respond.

A palm hits my left cheek. It stings as my body recoils from the shock, my mouth agape from the sudden reaction.

"Answer me!" The scream that leaves Chris's lips makes me jump. It's raw and powerful as his anger finally makes an appearance.

"No." I answer truthfully, the words barely a whisper as they leave my lips.

"Why not?" He recoils like I've hurt his feelings. "Is Detective Alvarez not fucking you good enough? It certainly looked like you were enjoying yourself."

Fire burns in my belly at his response. How dare he speak about the man who's done nothing but support me through the traumatic time he forced upon me? "Don't talk about him." I shake my head, my fearful face changing to fury.

"Don't tell me you've fallen for that protective crap?" His tone is resentful as he laughs at my response. "He does that to every case victim! You're not special to him, Saskia. You never will be." I ignore his words because I know they're not true, but that doesn't stop the bitter burn from scalding me. "But to me, you're more than special." Chris edges closer, the pad of his thumb brushing against my cheek.

"I'm not special to you," I hiss through my clenched jaw. "I'm just another toy that you think you can play with. But I'm not, and you can't."

He groans, rolling his eyes as he stands to his feet, throwing his hands up. "Look, those other girls," he waves it off. "They were just to pass the time until I could get my hands on you." Like a flash of lightning, he's crouching down in front of me, his rough palms holding my cheeks. "You're my puppet, Saskia. I'm going to play with you until I'm finished. I take whatever I want," his nose is flush against my ear as he takes a big inhale. "And you will give me all you have."

My body shakes violently, fear and adrenaline fighting for control. His breath so close to my skin fired warning signs inside of me, my body instantly attempting to recoil. I have no cards to play; I'm a helpless little lamb who's already on the defensive. I use the only threat I have. "Mitch will find me. You shouldn't have taken me when they're on high alert from that stupid picture!" I can't stop myself from raising my voice as my anger beams inside of me.

I don't have time to catch my breath before a thick hand is around my throat, squeezing my windpipe and cutting off my oxygen. His other hand disappears into his pocket, and he pulls out a gun, waving it around like it's a toy. "Detective Alvarez doesn't even know you're missing." He releases a long breath. "He still hasn't found his gun. What makes you think he'll find you before I have my way with you?"

His grip releases and I inhale a big gulp of air. My eyes focus on the sticker on the gun handle, Mitch's name written in cursive.

My worst thoughts fire through my mind.

He's going to kill me with Mitch's gun.

"You took it." The words come out as a statement instead of a question. I wasn't there when Mitch was shot, but heard what happened

"Yes. Well," he trails off. "Technically, no. I was laying low in that motel and dipped before the cops even arrived. I paid a junkie fifty-dollars to steal Detective Alvarez's gun." Inspecting Mitch's gun, he uses it to scratch his own head. "Turns out the junkie is ex-military. Knew how to sneak up on him and disarm him without getting hurt."

"Did you tell him to shoot Mitch, too?" I can barely catch my breath as I dread his response.

He shrugs, sarcasm plastered on his expression. "Well, yeah. I needed him out of the way."

Oh my god. My throat burns from the bile attempting to exit my stomach as the guilt pushes it up.

It's all my fault.

I can't stop the tears from falling.

"Don't cry, sweetheart." Chris's voice is patronising as he lifts my chin with Mitch's gun. "My plan didn't really work, did it." His laugh is humorless, but he plasters a fake smile on his scarred face. "You spent his recovery time in hospital with him, so I couldn't get to you. And when I was ready to try again, you went to his apartment and fucked him."

More hot tears carve their own path down my cheeks as the guilt overpowers me. I can barely even hear Chris's words over the sound of my pounding heartbeat.

"Stop crying." He's unbothered as he rolls his eyes. "Looked like a good time to me. I went to bed that night imagining it was me fucking you. Kept me hard all night."

I can't stop my stomach from expelling its contents on Chris's shoes, right in front of me. It burns my throat as I gag, the bitter taste cemented onto my taste buds.

"You bitch!" Chris growls as he glares at his shoes before turning his attention on me. I think he's going to slap or choke me again as his eyes turn black, but instead, the flash of metal out the corner of my eye makes my heart skip a beat.

Before I can even process what's happening, Mitch's gun strikes me across my face, and my vision blacks out as my surroundings blur into darkness.

Unconsciousness wasn't an option, but I never had a choice.

# 16

# MITCHELL

Peace of mind isn't possible when Saskia is a target. I'm concerned about her. She has a tendency to panic when something seems out of the ordinary, and when that happens, she needs someone in her corner to center her. How can I be there for her when she won't let me? The unanswered texts I've sent her tells me she needs her space, so I'm giving that to her, but I just want to know she's okay.

I hover outside the crime lab, waiting for any news on the picture snapped of me and Saskia. A tinge of embarrassment burns inside of me, as I watch my colleagues staring at the photo, then looking back at me. It's not subtle, but how many times do you see a work colleague with an erection, halfway entered inside a case victim?

She's not a goddamn case victim to me. That reminder instantly dissipates any embarrassment residing inside of me. That photo isn't an innocent mistake; it's an invasion of privacy. A chance to belittle Saskia and a statement to say the person who did this is still in control.

I have enemies, but usually they aim their anger at me. This was a personal, well thought out attack on me and Saskia. And there's only one person I know who would target her like this.

My phone buzzes in my pocket. Shoving my hand in to grab it, I look at the screen and frown at the caller ID. I swipe to answer. "Judge Donelly?" I answer, filled with unease.

"Detective Alvarez." Her tone has a sense of dread to it, and I don't like where this is going. "Is Saskia still at the station?"

There's a pit of terror in my stomach as her words soak in. It's like every single alarm has been raised inside of me because I know something is terribly wrong. "No?" It comes out as a question. "She left a couple hours ago. Why?" I ask, my voice wobbling slightly.

Judge Donelly sighs, and as I wait for her response, a piece of paper is handed to me from the crime lab. *Fingerprint match* is written in bold writing at the top, with a photo of a face I recognize all too well from the grainy tech photos.

Donald Hobbs.

Otherwise known as Chris on his dating profile.

Repeat offender for rape and kidnapping.

No permanent address for us to search.

*Fuck.*

"Mitch, are you there?" Judge Donelly's voice yanks me back to the present.

I don't bother asking her to repeat her sentence. "He's got her." The words are bitter as they leave my mouth.

I should have protected her. Stayed with her even when she didn't want me there. I knew Hobbs was out there somewhere. I'd rather her hate me and be safe than give her personal space, allowing her to be taken again.

But it's too late.

My feet carry me up the staircase faster than I can breathe. Each second feels like another tick on a time bomb. I shove past people coming the opposite way, not wasting time on apologizing or offering an explanation. I race through the main floor of the police station and head up the stairs to the detectives offices. The journey is gruelling as it reminds me I'll never be quick enough to keep her safe. My self hatred is pulling me back as its big hands wrap around my heart, but I can't give in to it right now. I can hate myself later.

Pushing the heavy doors to the department open with more vigor than necessary. I storm to Captain Wallace's office, Jules hot on my heels as she tries to ask me what's wrong.

Shoving my way through, I don't bother knocking on Captain Wallace's door as he sits at his desk on a phone call. His eyes are wide as he tries to tell me to leave, but one look at my panicked state is enough to say his goodbyes.

"He has Saskia." Acid burns my throat as my fists ball up. My anger is like electricity inside of me as it sparks at each thought of my girl.

"How do you know?" Captain Wallace rises to his feet, and I shove the fingerprint match document over to him.

Heading back out to the bullpen, all eyes are on me. "He's got Saskia and we need to find her." My hand swipes through my hair as I take a brief second to process what's happening. Jules steps up beside me, taking over for me. I thought I needed to be in control of this, but I trust my fellow detectives to do their jobs. "I'm going to follow her route she would have taken when she left here. Do whatever you need to," I point at them as I head towards the exit. "Just find her."

Standing outside the station, I take the route I saw Saskia walking earlier. Each step, I focus my eyes on the ground below me, searching for anything that is out of the ordinary or belongs to Saskia. Each step is another step towards defeat as doubt circles my mind.

Looking up at the courthouse, it's not hard to miss all of the security cameras, not to mention the ones across the street around the station. I shake my head, trying to find an explanation for this to make sense. Did he hold a gun to her which forced her to comply? How did he get her out of here without a struggle or witnesses? She disappeared from sight around here. I figured she walked in through the front, but there is a staff entrance around back. Surely she wouldn't go that way.

Heading down the alley, I realize this is most likely where he took her from. Searching around the area, I look for anything out of place or suspicious. Like the string of gold that catches my attention. I step closer and kneel down, to be faced with Saskia's cherry necklace.

My stomach sinks. He really does have her.

I dial Jules' number and put the phone to my ear. "Jules, I'm down the alley next to the courthouse, the staff entrance. Send the scene techs out here. I found some of Saskia's things."

"Okay." I hear her shouting something in the background. "Mitch," she pauses. "We're checking the security cameras now, we'll get her."

I squeeze my eyes shut. "I hope so." The words aren't filled with hope, though. The trepidation in my voice is obvious.

The wait for the scene techs is painful. I can't stop my mind counting the hours she's been with him as the sixth hour passes. The need to find Saskia is overwhelming but I can't leave our only piece of evidence for someone to contaminate, but I hate feeling helpless.

I see crime scene vans pull up the techs hop out with their suits and equipment in hand. Waving, I signal for them to hurry up so I can show them what I found.

The alleyway is taped off as a crime scene as the tyre marks and necklace are photographed. I run back up to my office to grab my car keys when Marten calls my name. I head over to his desk.

"I tracked Saskia's mobile, thankfully her GPS was turned on," he points at his computer screen. "Not even ten minutes after she left here, her phone was dropped or thrown, this is where it is now."

Both my hands find my head as panic claws at my insides. "She wasn't even out of my sight for two minutes." My words are barely a whisper as nausea churns my stomach. "Fuck!" I scream, my hands falling onto my hips.

"Mitch." Marten's hand is placed on my shoulder. "He planned this. He was watching her and knew when to take her. What do we know about him? Let's work with what we know," he says as he types. "OK, Donald Hobbs, let's see what we know about you."

"Thanks," I gently squeeze his shoulder. "I just need to find her."

"We will, man, we will. OK, so according to this he has a pretty nasty rap sheet. Petty theft, multiple assaults, attempted abductions, rape. He did 4 years for that one. He's been pretty quiet since his release, but he skipped out on his parole meeting and hasn't been seen since."

"Do we have an address for him? Where's he supposed to be staying?" I ask, needing to know more about this monster.

"He is supposed to be staying at a halfway house on the outskirts of town. Jules is already looking into it," he says.

"What about before prison, where did he grow up? Family? Known associates? Someone is helping him and he will need somewhere to keep Saskia." I say, the detective in me taking over.

"Alvarez!" Detective Hackett shouts. I turn around and see him holding up the phone, so I head over and press the loud-speaker button.

"Alvarez." I say as a greeting.

"Detective Alvarez?" The voice is soft, almost fake as their tone wobbles.

"Who is this?" I ask.

It's silent for a minute, followed by heavy breathing. It's haunting as the sound crawls up my skin and leaves goose-bumps in its place. I should hang up. We get the occasional prank call and this is exactly what they sound like, but something is telling me to keep the line open.

The anticipation is painful as we both wait each other out, but the silence between us is suddenly shattered as a bellowing, evil laugh echoes down the phone. I open my mouth to speak, but I'm cut off.

"Guess who it is." The voice is like gravel. It's rough and playful and their tone is low.

"I don't like guessing games." I say bluntly. I signal at Marten to track the location of the number calling, and he gives me a thumbs up as he starts typing.

"I guess you don't want to hear about the game I have planned then..." he trails off, dragging out the last syllable. "It's called 'how much can Saskia take?'"

"I swear to God, if you lay a single finger on her, I will kill you." My threat is an open flame as I grit through clenched jaws. Hobbs is toying with me.

"I should kill you for touching her." The sudden aggression in his tone tells me I've struck a nerve. "But I can't blame you. She is a fine piece of meat. We've had so much fun, well I have, I don't think Saskia enjoyed it much."

My eyes flick up to Marten as he spins his two index fingers around each other, telling me to keep Hobbs talking. This conversation is making me furious as my white knuckles desperately tempt me to put them through a wall.

"I'm going to make you pay for it. What do you want with her?" I ask the question, but I don't want to know the answer.

His chuckle is paralyzing. "I wanted to finish what I started...without the interruptions."

My vision is black as I process his words. I know what he does to women; I know exactly what's going to happen to Saskia and there's nothing I can do to fucking stop it.

I take a step away for a second as I pinch the bridge of my nose. I take a deep breath, trying to calm my mind, but images of Saskia flood through my brain. Every moment we've shared together plays on repeat in my mind, like my own self made torture device. I want to protect her. Pull her close to my chest and tell her everything is going to be okay.

Releasing a shaky breath, I try to compose myself. "Let me talk to her." I need to hear her voice. I need to know she's awake.

"Hm." Hobbs is blunt with his response. "Slight problem with that." His tone is sarcastic, and I want to reach through the phone and choke the life out of him for thinking this is a fucking game. "I taped her mouth shut because she spat at me." A sense of pride roars in my chest. "She can hear you though. You're on speaker. Tick tock."

I don't know if he's telling the truth or not, but I'm not wasting a moment if she can hear me. "Sas," I swallow a wad of saliva. "I'm coming for you, baby." The words feel like a bitter lie on my tongue. "Stay strong for me, cereza." I try to encourage her as I hear her soft cries. Pin pricks attack my chest as my heart shatters inside of me. I can barely hold it together as my hands shake and my voice quivers. "Stay strong for me, okay?"

Silence surrounds me as Hobbs ends the call, no doubt part of his sick fucking game.

I see red, anger boiling inside of me as my thumbs crack from clenched fists. "Tell me you got the location, Marten." I can barely speak above a whisper, but the poison in my tone burns as the words leave my mouth.

He taps keys on his keyboard frantically as the rest of the team gather around him, until he rises to his feet. "Got it! Five-eight-one-four Wellington Avenue. The houses on the street are all abandoned, the whole street is due for demolition."

I grab my car keys and head towards the exit, the rest of my team hot on my trail.

*I'm coming for you, baby.*

🍒 • 🍒 • 🍒 • 🍒

Wellington Avenue is everything I expected it to be. Gray, hollow and still. Homes here are boarded up and overgrown gardens. There isn't a single sign of life here as the wind whistles around us, sending us a warning to go home.

From our standpoint, I use binoculars to focus on our target. The windows are boarded up like the others, but it's the only home on this street with a mailbox. Dull blue paint decorates the two-storey home and a car sits in the driveway to the right.

I try to ground my mind as I strap on my bulletproof vest and check my ammo while the rest of the team readies around me. I slot my replacement gun into my holster and fasten it. I'm getting both my gun and Sas back today. I want to storm in and leave with Hobbs' head in my hands, but if we don't have a plan to follow through with, this could go horribly wrong and I'd lose Saskia. I'm not risking it. Patience is power when it's your only successor.

"Gather round." Captain Wallace signals over to him, the rest of the team following his lead. "I don't need to remind you of what's at stake here. Saskia is one of our own. Hobbs is a nasty piece of work so heads on a swivel. We don't know how many people are in there, so watch each other's backs..." Cap gives us our entry points but my focus slips back to the building. "Alvarez, I'm talking to you." Captain Wallace says.

"Sorry, Cap. All good here." I say.

"Look, Alvarez," Cap says, taking me aside. "I'm not sure it's a good idea that you go in there. Stay here with me, let Jules bring her out."

"I can't do that, Cap. Please don't bench me, I need this." I say with as much conviction as possible. The thought of waiting is unbearable.

"It's against protocol, you're too close to this, but I get it. Nothing on this earth could hold me back if my wife was in there, but I need you to be Detective Mitch Alvarez right now, not Mitch, Saskia's partner. You get me?" Cap says and I nod in understanding.

"I get it," I say.

"OK then, bring her home." Cap says with a nod.

We form up and make our way to the house, each entry team breaking off to their entry point. I follow Jules to the back door and we wait for the go signal through our earpieces.

"Go, go, go!"

As one we all breach, I force my foot against the back door, the thin plastic instantly snapping open. My mind is focused and I try to keep my breathing calm. It's hard to concentrate but I have to focus for Saskia's sake.

Shouting from the rest of the team echoes through the dark, dusty home. Dirty dishes litter the kitchen side and old newspaper is used to cover the flooring as old belongings lay around on any surface they can find. Everywhere I step is a pile of faeces, but I keep my gun up and search for any movement. We head down a narrow hall, the scent of urine invades my nostrils as I try not to gag. There's little to no lighting, but there should be a basement door around here. After trying one door and finding the source of the urine, we try the last door. I jiggle the door handle, but it doesn't budge, so I lift my foot and kick the door, the loud thump loosening the rusted lock and nudging the hinges. With another kick, it flies open and pounds on the wall behind it as a shower of dust scatters into the musty air.

"Saskia?" I shout as I run down the creaking stairs. We know this is the most likely location to keep her. With barely any light I lift my torch and swing the arc of light around.

My eyes wince at the brightness, as well as the hundreds of dust particles polluting the air. I look around, taking in the rundown wallpaper and decaying red carpet. This room is underground. It's quiet and inaccessible unless you're in the home. It's the perfect room for a kidnapper.

The chains on the wall and more than one mattress on the floor catch my eye as I take a closer look, my stomach contents threatening to expel. This is his sex dungeon. Various tools, implements and sex toys lay around the floor. Panic blares inside of me as realization crashes into me.

Has he used these on Saskia?

I'm about to explode as rage pours gasoline on my lit match, my body tensing up from the absolute fucking horror that is this room, but my mind has other ideas, I feel like I'm in a daydream as my mind tries to convince me Saskia is safe and this is just another bust. Everything is okay...

"Mitch..." Jules shouts, pulling me from my head, she's crouching down but moving in slow motion. Suddenly the world speeds up again as I realize what she's saying. "...for fuck sake Mitch! Pull your shit together and help me!"

Moving around her, I realize someone is lying on the mattress in front of Jules. My mind still not working at full capacity, I crouch down to see who it is and how I can help. Jules is frantically calling on the radio. Toned legs, littered with bruises and ligature marks, underwear - Saskia had the same underwear on this morning and I smile at the memory. It's like my mind was protecting itself and the sight of her underwear shattered the illusion. I drop to my knees as my heart sinks with me, the intense pain in my chest almost paralyzing me. "Sas, baby," I sweep a stray curl from her forehead. I pull my pocket knife out and begin cutting the rope restraints, the gut-wrenching sense of deja vu falling over us. Her unconscious body lays limp in my arms as I scoop her up. I rise to my feet and tuck her close to my chest before I begin heading up the stairs.

"Mitch." Jules calls out behind me as she follows up the stairs. She holds her radio up to me. "That was Cap. They've caught Hobbs. They're on their way to the station."

I nod, a sense of relief washing over me, but it diminishes the second I look at Saskia. Once again, she'll be waking up in a hospital bed after the way this man violated her.

Murder isn't the right answer, but sometimes it's the right thing to do.

# 17

# SASKIA

I'd hoped I wouldn't be laying in a hospital bed, staring aimlessly at the ceiling, after being taken by my stalker again, but here I am. I feel so numb, like my signals from my brain are being blocked by survival mode. I'm free from Donald Hobbs physical torture, but I don't know if I'll ever truly be free of him. Thankfully, the nurses collected as much physical evidence from me as possible. DNA from under my fingernails, ligature marks from my restraints, a rape kit. I think that was the hardest part, but I'm glad they did it.

As more bruises appear, they come and take more photos. I don't think I've ever had so many photos taken before.

"All done." The nurse says as she places her hand gently on my bicep. "Do you want me to send Detective Alvarez back in?"

I nod, forcing a smile onto my face. Everyone is treating me like a broken doll and I hate it. I know why, and I don't blame them, but I'm sick and tired of being the victim. Donald Hobbs has turned me into a coward, flinching at anything that catches my attention. I don't want to live like that. He's in police custody and he's going to stay there until he goes to jail, because I'm going to stand up in court and tell everyone what he's done to me, physically and mentally. I was awake for a lot of it, although it felt like it was happening to someone else. I've listened to victims in court talk about the mind and body separation and I get it now.I deserve better than what he put me through, and I won't let him get away with it.

The door clicks open, and for a brief second, I panic. But my fear dissipates when I hear that soothing voice.

"Hey baby." Mitch walks over towards me faster than he needs to, his hair dishevelled and dark circles beginning to appear under his eyes. "Are you okay?" He asks, but I know he's not talking about my general wellness. He's referring to the evidence collecting ordeal.

I nod. "It was fine. Are you okay?" I ask, and he instantly knows I'm not asking about his wellness either. He's not slept since I was kidnapped. Probably not even eaten. God knows when his last drink was.

"Don't worry about me, cereza." He hums gently, taking a seat next to me and grasping my hand. His touch is cool, but reassuring. "I'm fine."

I don't believe him, but I'm not pushing him any further. Instead, I take in his features. His small crease in between his eyebrows. The stubble pushing through around his chin. Those brown eyes that suck me in whenever I look into them. I want to gaze into those oak irises everyday as I let every single problem wash away.

"What are you thinking about?" Mitch's index finger rubs soft circles on my cheek as his cheeks lift up into a sweet smile.

I shrug, my mind still focused on how I want to spend my mornings. "You." I tell him, unable to look him in the eye as shyness engulfs me.

"Me?" His tone is shocked as he recoils slightly, but that playful smile only grows bigger. "Goddamn." He brushes his fingers through his hair. "Saskia Hernandez," my name sounds like sex on his lips. "Are you trying to make me blush?"

"Did it work?" I squint.

"Of course it did." He nods, pulling my hand to his lips and kissing it. "You don't even have to try, cereza."

My stomach blooms as he speaks. His words fall off his lips so naturally, like he doesn't need to exaggerate to get his point across. And I believe every single word that falls from those perfect lips.

Ringing interrupts our conversation as Mitch sighs, his eyes rolling. He doesn't look at his phone, but he knows it's his as he lets it ring in his pocket. The call cuts off and he offers me an apologetic smile, but it's quickly changed to a wince as his phone rings again.

"What's up?" I ask, my gut sinking at his dissatisfaction with the calls.

"Nothing. It's-" Mitch begins, checking his watch before looking at me gently. "It's Jules. Hobbs is in interrogation and my opportunity to question him is nearly gone."

Anxiety churns in my stomach at the thought of Mitch being in the same room as that monster while flashbacks of what he's capable of assaults my vision. But Mitch is stronger than me. This is his job, the thing he's dedicated so much of his adult life to. I can't stop him from doing it, just because the criminal he's questioning is the one who violated me.

"Go." I tell him, nodding for extra reassurance. "I'll be fine."

I expected him to get up and go, but he doesn't move. Soft features stare at me as silence balances around us. "I don't want to let you out of my sight again." He shakes his head, and I swear I see a thick pool of water on his lash line, but he suddenly looks down and blinks.

"I'll be in the exact same place when you come back." I try to convince him. "Anyway, Hobbs will be with you, not me. I'm safe here."

"But if something does-" He starts, but I don't allow him to finish that sentence.

"Mitch." My tone is stern as I widen my eyes at him, hoping there's some sort of authority in my state.

"I would never forgive myself, Sas. I don't forgive myself. I just need you safe." He whispers the last part as his voice cracks, and I think my heart does at the same time. It's painful watching someone you care about beat themselves up over something that isn't their fault.

"It's not your fault." I shake my head and squeeze his hand. He can barely look at me, and that's what hurts the most. That he thinks this is his fault and I'm the product of his failure. "None of this is your fault, Mitch."

He shakes his head, his eyes heavy as defeat weighs them down. He pulls out his phone and begins texting as he keeps constant hold of my hand. It's like he's afraid to let go, in case I slip out of his vision again.

Pocketing his phone, he rises to his feet and straightens his shirt as he releases a long breath. "I'm going to speak to the officers on watch outside your door." He looks down at me as he sweeps a stray curl from my forehead. "I need to know they're trustworthy."

I don't argue with him. It's the only way he'll trust that I'm safe here, especially after last time's ordeal with cops on watch.

I can't hear their conversation, but I can hear Mitch's stern voice. I count myself lucky that I have never been a suspect on the end of his interrogation. I've seen Mitch in court and his abilities to control each situation is why he's got so many positive outcomes in his cases.

A nurse comes by with some more IV pain medication, and I give her a nod to let her know I'm ready. As she's injecting, Mitch enters the room with Detective Marten right behind him, a paper in one hand and a coffee in another. I frown, confused about what's going on and why there's two detectives here when their suspect is at their police station.

"Marten is going to sit with you while I go to the station. There are cops outside the door." Mitch leans down, his lips hovering above mine, so close that I can feel the heat from his breath. "I'm just a call away if you need me, okay, cereza?"

I nod, barely able to take in his words as his lips distract me. But he doesn't kiss me. Instead, he places a warm kiss on my forehead before giving my hand one last squeeze. I blink and he's out of the door in a flash.

As each second ticks by, my mind gets foggier as the pain medication begins kicking in, sending me into drowsiness as my consciousness fades.

# Mitchell

I'm going to kill the bastard.

I know this is a terrible idea, but I can't allow him to move on without knowing the damage he's inflicted. I stand outside the interrogation room as Captain Wallace stands beside me, watching Jules and Hackett question Hobbs. "May I?" I point to the room as I turn my head towards Cap, asking for permission. I should stay and observe from a distance, but I want to see his face up close, just so I can see the fear of a life sentence on his disgusting face.

He offers me a nod before turning his attention back to the one way window.

The metal door squeaks as I push it open, my eyes instantly setting on Hobbs. He offers me a slight smile, but I know there's nothing genuine about it. He thinks he can use me as a toy, just like he's used to doing. But not the same way he used Saskia. He can use me as a power play, to push my buttons and get a rise out of me.

But I can't fall that far. I *need* to keep composure.

Calming my mind, I glance around the square, brick room. The walls are painted black and the windows on the back walls are barred up. The wall behind me is the only exit and entry point, with a large one way mirror on the left wall, perfectly positioned in front of the table, fitted with handcuffs. It's cold as the walls offer no insulation, and the smell of must is a constant in this room, but I've gotten used to it.

"I'm not telling you anything." Hobbs rests his chin on his hand, a satisfied smirk plastered on his smug face. I noticed his stuck pinky finger, exactly how Saskia explained it.

"We spoke to your boss at Wellington Farm. He said you've sustained a few injuries in your time as an employee." Hackett spreads out medical reports of Hobbs documented injuries. "The exact same injuries victims reported our serial rapist having."

Hobbs scoffs and looks away, hiding his pinky underneath his other hand. "What can I say? They have it wrong."

"No, Donald." Jules shakes her head, leaning down in front of him. "The person they described is you." She points a finger in his face, causing an immediate reaction from him as he grits his teeth and frowns at her. I can see he's using every ounce of self control to not blow up at Jules from his white knuckles as clenched jaw.

"We have answers and evidence for every single question a jury will want answered." Hackett shrugs, plopping down the numerous case files on Hobbs. He has seven victims, including Saskia. Seven women who have been violated by this sick excuse of a human being.

I inhale and exhale slowly, attempting to calm some of the anger inside of me. I won't allow myself to give in to his devious games.

"You can refuse to talk to us, Hobbs, but it won't do you any good." Jules takes a seat opposite Hobbs in an attempt to get him to speak. She's a female and he views them as inanimate. An object for him to toy around with when he feels like it. A puppet to keep him in control. It's his weakness.

Hobbs internally deliberates for a second as he keeps his eyes set on Jules, before he lifts his head. "What do I get in return?" He's bargaining. *Pathetic.*

"A plea." Her tone is blunt as she rests her elbows on the table. A plea is an easy way out, but it stops a trial from going ahead and those women, including Saskia, from reliving that hell over again.

"Hmm," Hobbs taps his finger on the table as he looks around the room. He seems to be considering it, and as the seconds tick by painfully slow, I silently pray it's an opportunity he'll take. "Pass." He shrugs casually. "I'd like another opportunity to look at my sweetheart, Saskia, again."

"And what makes her so special that you had to take her a second time?" Hackett keeps his cool, baiting Hobbs into proving he's guilty, which is much better than I'm doing. I'm fighting an internal battle to keep myself routed and not react to anything Hobbs says. "Why toy with Detective Alvarez and take Saskia?" Hackett questions, sitting in front of Hobbs as he focuses on him.

"There's something about her..." Hobbs trails off, aimlessly looking around the room like he's lost in thought. "She intrigued me. And when she got involved with Detective Alvarez," he leans closer to Hackett, squinting his eyes and smirking, "and I mean *involved*," he backs up. "It infuriated me. She's not his to touch. She's mine." I can see his words barely seeping through his grit teeth. I'm a tender topic for him.

Hobbs leans back and relaxes, his shoulders dropping as he slouches in the metal chair. "She fights back, I like that. Every time I see her, my mind pictures her getting fucked by you, Detective Alvarez. She took you so well. No wonder you gave in to that fine piece of meat." The grin on his face is menacing.

My veins burst with fury as my body fires with electricity. I force a deep breath to enter my lungs, but instead I use it as fuel as I storm towards Hobbs. My hand finds its way around his throat as I squeeze against his dull skin, his pulse throbbing against my fingers. My mouth skims his ear as I fight every ounce of self restraint inside of myself to not bite a chunk of his flesh. "If you ever mention Saskia's name again, I will gouge out your eyeballs and pour bleach in your mangled eye sockets, as I watch you scream like a pathetic little bitch."

My hand shakes around his throat, tempting me to squeeze harder, but the tap on my back pulls me back to reality. Meeting Hobbs helpless eyes...Cap shakes my shoulder and I realize I was daydreaming, I'm still standing in the viewing room. Fuck that was intense.

"So," Jules leans forward with her palms on the table, intimidation clear in her wide posture. "You're giving up your chance for a lighter sentence, just to see Saskia in court?" She squints at him, but Hobbs just nods in return.

*Son of a bitch.*

Jules proceeds. "Tell me, how did you encrypt your profile photo so securely? I can't imagine a man like you has that kind of knowledge."

His laugh is menacing with no concern for the situation he's in. "I found someone on a hacking forum online. I dropped the money off to a P.O. Box and they sent me the final photo."

My fists throb from the intense pressure. There are parts of me that I didn't even consider using as a weapon. My mind flashes with gruesome ways to hurt Hobbs, just so he suffers in a way that he could only experience in the most paralysing nightmare.

"The hotels and storage rooms." Hackett flips a piece of paper around with Hobbs frequent locations where he would keep his victims. "Why leave your victims there for hours?"

"I had work to attend to." He waves his hand nonchalantly, like it was an obvious answer. "Then, I'd have to get them to the basement without Doris seeing. She's too old to be experiencing that kind of stress."

I scoff a laugh, but there's no humor in it. He cares for one woman, but not others. How can he consider his childhood carer's feelings, yet completely disregard others? Using her basement to commit heinous crimes while she's one floor above, without any concern to the woman he's brutalising. But he's worried about the ninety-year-old woman who can barely hear and see.

Fucking psychopath.

Hobbs' voice is a shattered disruption in the interrogation room. "Where is she, anyway? I guess I better get one more good look in, then...I need a mental image to wank over in jail."

A deep breath in.

And a deep breath out.

Eyes closed to center myself.

"Put him in the cells." I say through grit teeth towards Captain Wallace before walking away from the interrogation room. I need a minute to calm down and center myself, to get my head in the game and focus on justice the right way.

But my feet take me to the basement where the cells are kept. Closed off rooms with a metal bed and a thin blanket, and one full cup of water. Enough to keep an offender going until they are released or taken to jail. One clueless member of staff on the desk that has their headphones on most of the time and no cameras. It's goddamn perfect.

I stand outside the cell at the end of the hallway, checking the cell next door to make sure it's empty. My legs itch to pace up and down as time moves painfully slowly, but I fight the urge.

Distant chatter echoes down the hall as I faintly hear Jules checking Hobbs in. Hobbs' obnoxious voice gets louder as Hackett gives blunt responses, not engaging in the conversation that Hobbs so desperately wants. They narrow the hallway and I see Hobbs shoulders tense up at the sight of me, but he forces them back down.

"Are you lost?" Hobbs smirks as he looks at Jules for her encouragement, but she doesn't react.

"I'm exactly where I need to be." I answer, unlocking the thick metal cell door and walking in. Hobbs is pushed in by Hackett, as he and Jules stand at the door, watching. I should make this fair and take off his cuffs, but he deserves the same treatment he gave Saskia and the other victims.

"Key." I hold my hand out at Jules and she passes over the handcuff key. I force Hobbs down onto the bed, yank his arms towards the end, and unlock one wrist. Looping the metal under the bed bar, I grab his wrist and lock it back into the handcuff, chucking the key back to Jules.

"Just so you know," my arms crossed over my chest. "A promotion from being a cop doesn't land you the position of deputy." I shrug. "You fucked your own plan from lack of knowledge."

Hobbs frowns but recognition sparks in his features. "Yeah, well, I got enough. More than enough, in fact. I've ruined her for you." His grin is sinister, and I can't stop the sadistic smile from growing on my face.

"Stage a power cut." I turn to my left, looking at Hackett. He doesn't question my demand, instead, he gives a small head nod and leaves with no further questions.

"What's happening?" Hobbs questions, metal clanking against metal as he tries to shake his handcuffs free. It's the first time I've heard fear in his voice, and I fucking revel in it.

I ignore him as I shut the door behind me, peering at Jules through the small window of thick bars. She locks the door from the outside and stands against the wall.

"A power cut?" Hobbs' voice wobbles as he panics, but I don't see the fear in his eyes, because the electricity cuts in the cell. Dull, blue, emergency fixture lights flick on, offering us an ounce of brightness of the original lights, as Hobbs' outline becomes a black mass in front of me. Like it's my target, he's my sole focus as my surroundings whittle away.

"Not a power cut." I growl, prowling towards his jittering body, looking down on him. "Punishment." I tell him matter-of-factly.

He opens his mouth to respond, but I don't give him the opportunity, like he never gave his victims the opportunity to say no. My fist clashes with his jaw, a loud crack echoing throughout the small room. He leans forward and coughs as thick, red liquid spills from his mouth, gurgling some kind of refusal.

I punch him again, this time on the other cheek, knocking a tooth loose as he spits it out mid cough. He dribbles blood and saliva as it gathers on his trousers below him, as he sits helpless and restrained. I can't help but chuckle at the irony.

"Please stop!" He begs, blood spatters landing on my white shirt. *Inconsiderate.*

"Like you did?" I tilt my head, straightening my lips. "No." I tell him plainly as I pull him to the floor. He kneels in front of the bed, his hands still restrained as I circle around the back of him.

My fingers find his thin hair strands, wet with sweat and grease. I pull his scalp hard enough to hear his whimpers, before slamming his face onto the bed frame. The thud vibrates the floor, yet it's fucking satisfies me. I lift his head backwards and admire my work as blood pools from his mouth and nose, his front teeth chipped or missing. He can't even form a sentence as he gargles on his own blood, but I'm already sick of seeing his face, so I slam it down on the bed again.

Again.

Again.

And again.

Until my vision is black with rage and my muscles ache with satisfaction.

I don't hear the cell door unlock, but I'm being pulled off of Hobbs, his face mangled and disfigured and his skin not visible through the maroon liquid covering him. His body slumped over the bed frame as he wheezes, pathetic attempts to beg for his life.

Paralyzing fear never looked so goddamn good.

If getting some form of justice for Saskia makes me a monster, then I'm a goddamn nightmare. No one hurts my girl and lives pain free after the hell they caused. My actions were his consequence and I happily delivered his karma.

🍒 • 🍒 • 🍒 • 🍒

Pulling a sleeping Saskia into my side, I readjust myself on her hospital bed so we can both fit. After a hot shower and some time to cool down, I snuck back into the hospital just so I could feel Saskia breathing against my chest. I hope she never finds out what really happened in that interrogation room. I'm not a violent man, but I'm a violent animal when it comes to protecting those who I love.

*Love.*

That's the swelling in my heart and the butterflies in my stomach. The dominating need to protect her with everything I have. The constant fear of not being able to be her savior.

Gently placing a kiss on her forehead, I brush my finger down her cheek. I inhale her scent as cherry and orchid scent invades my nostrils and memorize each freckle on her face.

"God, I love you, Sas." I whisper against her soft curls, careful not to wake her. I soak up every second of the calm moments with my cereza safe in my arms and the threat locked in a jail cell.

It feels like peace is slowly filtering around us as this hell comes to an end. Saskia deserves a life of serenity. One where she can walk down the street without someone following her.

One where her home doesn't need to be watched by cops constantly. One where she has me by her side, to love and protect her. *Hopefully.*

"I love you, too, Mitch." For a moment I thought I hallucinated Saskia's gentle voice, but as I peer down, her sleepy eyes are looking up at me, hope swimming in her brown irises. She interlocks her warm hands with mine and nestles her head into my shoulder, before closing her eyes again.

I fight every urge inside of me to not jump up and fucking scream as elation vibrates my body.

She fucking loves *me.*

The smile on my face is never fucking disappearing.

# 18

# SASKIA

Therapy is gruelling and I leave every session drained. I have to attend three times a week as part of my recovery. I told Judge Donelly three sessions a week wasn't necessary, but she insisted. Mitch takes me and waits for me to finish, so he can take me to get cherry gelato afterwards. He doesn't push me to talk or completely changes the subject. He just lets me make the conversation so he knows I'm comfortable.

It's barely been three weeks since I was rescued and the trial is already coming to an end. Judge Donelly brought it forward so it could be an open and shut case. She's carried me throughout my recovery so far, along with Mitch, and I don't think I would've made it out of the hospital without their help. She made sure Hobbs stayed locked up in jail, with no bail until the trial. She's demanded the best lawyer in Casamount to fight our case. All 7 of his victims agreed to stand up and testify in court, it was hard listening to the horrors he put these women through. Standing up to Hobbs at trial is the most terrifying thing about proving his guilt, but with all those fighting our corner, I'm optimistic about this case.

"You ready?" Mitch places his palm out in front of me as his standing figure looms over my sitting one. We are at the courthouse, waiting for the jury to finish deliberating Hobbs' guilt. This building has always been a space of comfort for me, but right now, it's a slice of hell.

I grasp Mitch's hand and he lightly pulls me to my feet. He pulls me in close and places a soft kiss on my forehead, before interlocking his fingers into mine.

For me to have the best chance at winning this case, Mitch had to recuse himself as an investigator. I'm not sure what exactly happened the morning after I was rescued. All I know is Hobbs' injuries were sustained in prison when he first got there. That's the story that was put on the official police report. The security cameras went down when the power stopped working that night, so there's no one to prove otherwise. Whether that's the truth or not, I don't care to find out. He deserved every blow he received, and whoever landed those is my angel in the form of revenge.

Truth be told, I know exactly who did it. And I think no different of him. In fact, it only makes me admire him more for doing what I couldn't.

And it's worked out perfectly. Mitch still has his job, he's not a suspect for what happened to Hobbs and I came out safe on the other end. Of course Mitch not being able to fight this case isn't great, but he's still working it, off the record. He plainly refused to recuse himself fully. He wouldn't allow his colleagues to solve this without him, especially with his personal stake in the situation.

Entering the all wooden courtroom, we take a seat in the front row alongside the other plaintiffs and Mitch's colleagues and behind my lawyer, Lenora, who's fighting my case. I've sat at the front of this exact courtroom hundreds of times, yet I've never felt the spotlight as much as I have during this trial. The constant sideways stares from onlookers, the jury's curious glances and the paralyzing glares from Hobbs himself. I don't have to look in his direction to know his attention is on me. My body senses his eyes in my direction as my hairs stand on edge. There's an ice cold shiver that skates down my spine like a warning. But Mitch doesn't let him stare for long.

I notice his cough and hand through hair action in sync, and so does Judge Donelly, as she picks up on his cue and directs Hobbs to look forward.

I feel exposed and bare in front of every single attendee in this courtroom. They've combed through my life and judged every inch of it; the prosecution coming up with their own thoughts and theories while they try to make me the bad guy. They watched me breakdown on the stand as I recounted every horrifying detail Hobbs put me through. My once private life has been displayed to many of Casamount's residents as they learn things about me that I never intended to tell them.

This is what Hobbs wanted. He knew we'd push for justice, but at what cost? My business is now everyone's as they soak up and revel in the gossip of my life. But I *had* to do this. For me. For every victim of a stalker who won't take no for an answer. Justice is still *justice*.

Whispers and gasps fill the packed courtroom as Judge Donelly instructs everyone to stand before the court. Doing as instructed, I rise to my feet, Mitch's hand interlocked with mine as he rubs reassuring circles on my hand. The jury enters the room and takes their seats as one member stays standing.

"Have the jury reached a verdict?" Judge Donelly's voice is strong as she lowers her glasses lightly.

Anxiety churns my stomach as my ears throb to block out the noise. I don't know if I want to hear their response as my hands shake in fear. I've fought so much for this case, and for it to not go the way I wanted would completely shatter me.

"We have, your Honor." The lead juror announces as she holds a small stack of papers in her hands. Her eyes hover above the words as she waits for Judge Donelly's signal.

My heartbeat is nearing my sternum as it pumps so loudly, I think I may just pass out. I can't deal with the tense pressure building in this room as nausea threatens to make an appearance.

Mitch's hand snakes around my back as he pulls me close, with Jules' hand squeezing mine for reassurance.

"How do you find the defendant?" Judge Donelly instructs. I can faintly see her thrumming pulse in her neck, and I find relief in her apprehension.

"We, the jury," she clears her throat. "Find Donald Hobbs, the defendant, guilty on all counts."

*Guilty.*

He's fucking guilty.

I can't stop the tears from leaking down my face as the man who took all my choices away is now going to face the same fate. Karma is a dish best served on a cold prison plate and that's the exact meal Hobbs is going to be eating.

I'm stuck in a bubble of elation as we leave the courtroom, but it's immediately popped by the amount of flashing cameras outside the main doors. I'm overwhelmed, sleep deprived and still terrified to speak of the man who almost ruined my life. Dread tries to drag me down as my breathing picks up, but Mitch grabs my hand and leads me to an area of the court that is off limits to the public.

A small grass area outside Judge Donelly's office with pink blossom trees either side. It's beautiful and private, a small piece of heaven in the chaos that's surrounding us.

I'm too focused on the delicate petals falling from the trees like snowfall that I don't feel Mitch behind me until he's flush against my back. I turn my head sideways to look at him, but before I get a chance, he holds a bunch of red lilies in front of me with a small handwritten note.

*I'm so proud of you. I love you.*

A riot of butterflies swarm my stomach, my body reacting to words this man says like a chemical reaction inside of me. Containing my emotions feels impossible when Mitch makes me feel so seen. Bliss does truly exist when understanding is a form of affection.

Leaning forward, I take a deep inhale of the beautiful blooms, before turning around to face him. "Tell me again." I hum, my cheeks lifting as I peer up at him.

He holds the flowers forward for me to take and takes a step forward. His eyes focus on mine, dipping to my lips in between glances. His warm palms find my cheeks as he bites back a smile. "Saskia Hernandez. I'm so fucking proud of you," he lowers his lips to mine, gently skimming my flesh. "And I love you so goddamn much that my heart aches." His voice vibrates against my mouth, like a temptation luring me in.

I have to bite my tongue to not kiss him right now. So I soak in his words instead, playing them on repeat in my mind as my smile grows into a full blown grin. "Well, Detective Alverez, I appreciate your honesty." I tease him, stepping back and turning to walk away. I don't get far as my body is wooshed backwards and pulled flush against his. Heat and rapid breathing lights a fire between us as our lips keep the smallest gap between them.

"I'd appreciate yours." He breathes, his thumb caressing my cheek. "Unless you want things to go back to the way they were before."

"No." I say embarrassingly fast. "I don't. I need you."

"Need me, huh?" He hums, a teasing smirk pulling at his lips.

I nod. "I want you. I need you. And I fucking love you, too, Mitchell Alvarez."

An explosion of emotions erupt inside my stomach as Mitch crashes his lips to mine, explaining everything he's feeling in the way he kisses. He's dominant, but soft and reassuring at the same time. It's hot and sexy as he takes control of me, and I fully trust him with the wheel.

His lips skim my ear, his voice a soft whisper as he speaks. "I was hoping you'd say that, because you revived the dead feeling of hope inside of me. My life was dull before I met you. Now it's every shade of red, because that's you. My cereza, my cherry, my Saskia. Mi amor."

The only reason I made it out of this alive was because of Mitch. He saved me. My pillar of support when I'm unable to stand by myself.

He restored justice for me.

And I restored love for him.

# Epilogue

## SASKIA

**ONE YEAR LATER**

"Kiwi!" I shake the bowl of fish, trying to get his attention. With no avail, I grab the bag of cat treats and shake them for a few seconds, and low and behold, gray paws begin strolling in through the cat flap. He looks at me expectantly, waiting for his treats, so I place a couple in his bowl, but I can't resist giving him a cuddle before he eats. Lifting him up, he nuzzles his head into my neck as he purrs his delight. I suddenly feel guilty for leaving him with Indie for the week. "Mamá and papá are heading to España for the week. You be good for Aunt Indie."

He wriggles free of my hold and goes straight to his food bowl, and I realize he didn't listen to a single word I said. Sighing, I finish packing my suitcase and check off a few more items on my list.

Our lives went back to normality a few weeks after the sentencing. I was shot a few stares and glares from passersby, but I got used to it. It soon stopped happening as I turned into old news and the next Casamount story became the center of attention. After a couple of months of intense therapy, I was finally able to drop my sessions to once a week. I keep up regular sessions so I have a safe space to discuss anything on my mind. Like how abnormal my life felt after the kidnapping. How I still didn't feel safe after Hobbs was jailed. And how this intense feeling of adoration took over my heart for Mitch.

We took things slow as we both adjusted to normal life again, but we spent those few months so close that we became each other's other half. It didn't take us long to become exclusive and become cat parents after finding a sweet stray lingering around the courthouse. We named him Kiwi after his obsession with the fruit, and he very quickly settled into my home. Which led us onto our next decision; moving in. It was hard being cat parents when we didn't live together, so we took the leap and went with it. We settled on my place because Kiwi is comfortable here. Mitch sold his apartment and spent some of the money on a really expensive security system for our home. He can relax knowing I'm safe and I'm safe because he's protecting me. Mitch soothes every wound I have, and he takes it upon himself to fix the issue. I no longer have to face this big, scary world alone. One day he was just a detective across the courtroom, and it blossomed into the other half of my soul.

Fate planned for us to cross paths.

Destiny cemented our future together.

And my God, it's a beautiful future we have planned.

## Mitchell

Sweltering heat engulfs me as the sun beams above us. But I'm more concerned at how my dick keeps reacting to Saskia in her red dress. The fabric is tight around her perfect tits and flows out on the lower half, leaving me to imagine her plump ass and perfect pussy below. We have the most breathtaking views as we have the vineyard to ourselves, looking onto the mountains with a cotton candy sunset. Yet, she's still the most ethereal thing I've ever seen.

We spent the afternoon wine tasting some of Spain's most delicious wines, before taking a stroll through the acres of land.

With a wine bottle in one hand and Saskia's hand in the other, we stroll down to the bottom of the vineyard, into a floral corner. Entering the dahlia covered archway, we're met with a large mirror against one bush, with perfect floral arrangements on the other three. It looks like an art installation, it's beautiful. The flowers act as a view blocker so inside the petals, you're in privacy.

Saskia takes a seat on one of the white chairs that face the mirror as she looks at her reflection.

"What do you see?" I ask her, placing the wine on the second chair as I circle behind her.

She shrugs. "I don't know." Her eyes meet mine in the mirror, soft and dainty, she offers a small smile.

I shake my head and gently pull her curls from the front of her face to behind, so they fall down her back. "I see perfection." I place a soft kiss on her delicate neck, her skin instantly reacting to me. It took a lot of time and patience for Saskia to feel comfortable with touch again.

"Not quite." She shrugs, her neck tilted to the side as she waits for another kiss, but I don't give it to her.

Instead, I yank the zip down on her dress. She yelps, but doesn't move to correct it, so I circle around the front of her. "Take it off." I say sternly, offering her a hand to help her stand.

She takes it, as she slowly rises, never breaking eye contact with me. Leisurely, Saskia drops one strap after the other, and allows the dress to fall to the floor in a perfect bunch. She steps out of it and moves it to the side. Her trust in me completely blows me away every time she places herself at my mercy. She knows I'll always keep her safe.

In nothing but her panties, my eyes fall to her breasts, her nipples pebbled and waiting for me. I take a step closer, anticipation thick between us as I inhale her gorgeous cherry scent. Looping my fingers into her waistband, I lower her panties down her legs, and wait for her to step out of them before I shove them in my slacks pocket.

She stands bare and beautiful in front of me, her cheeks flushed and the fast rise and fall of her chest. "Sit." I direct, nodding to the chair behind her. She follows my instructions as she lowers to sit, a quick inhale as her bare ass touches the cool material. I drop to my knees in front of her and open her thighs, her pussy glistening in front of me. "Watch yourself." I tell her, pointing to the mirror behind me as I grab the wine bottle. Her eyebrows pull together slightly as her curiosity builds but she waits patiently. I unscrew the bottle cap and hold the deep red wine above us. Slowly, I tip the bottle so the wine trickles down her folds. She gasps as the cool liquid assaults her sex, but desire pushes her legs further apart.

Putting the wine bottle down on the table, I wrap my hands under her thighs and pull her closer to me. "See how fucking perfect you look while I eat your pussy." My instruction is clear, and as soon as her eyes fall onto her naked figure in the mirror, my tongue swipes from entrance to clit, licking up the drops of wine. I swallow what I could gather before diving back into her clit. Flicking and sucking, I eat like I haven't had a meal in days as I savor her sweet taste.

She moans and gasps as her hands get lost in my hair, but she never takes her attention off herself in the mirror. "That's my good girl." I hum, my words vibrating her pussy. "Watching yourself like you were told."

She bucks against my face, her eyes struggling to stay open as she silently pleads for more. I return to my feast between her legs, teasing her entrance with finger, I slowly push it in, revelling in her groan as she nibbles on her bottom lip. I pump and lick at a constant pace, her moans of satisfaction playing like a song on repeat.

Adding another finger, her legs move further apart as I lift one onto my shoulder. Her pussy is so fucking addicting, prying me off of her is harder than travelling to space. I'd die between these thighs if I had the choice.

"Oh my God." She whines, grinding on my face.

"God?" I tease. "Don't insult me, baby. He couldn't handle your sweet pussy riding his face."

Without warning, her head falls back as her toes curl, her moans goddamn hypnotic. She thrusts against my tongue faster, riding through her orgasm. My fingers inside of her are slick with her juices as she throbs around them. I don't waste a single drop as I withdraw slowly and place them in my mouth, savoring her flavor.

I rise to my feet, looking down on her flustered figure as mischief fills her face. I follow her eyes to my erection, her hands already attempting to unbutton my slacks. She gets there eventually and lowers them. Turning me around, she pulls my hands down to sit in her seat. Lifting my shirt over my head, she drops to her knees as she pins me with alluring eyes. "Watch yourself or watch me take your cock. You choose." Her voice drips with seduction, and I have to fight the urge to come right here.

Wrapping her fist around my cock, her tongue darts out and licks up my length, from bottom to top. "Fuck." I growl, clenching my teeth to control myself.

She takes my dick in her mouth and begins sucking, and every inch of my being feels like I'm levitating. I can barely keep my eyes open as she sucks and licks, moving her right hand up and down in unison. Her left hand finds my balls as she cups them, leaving no area of skin untouched. I can't take my eyes off of her, as her cheeks hollow out and her eyes begin watering, with fat tears carving lines down her cheeks.

"So fucking perfect." I utter as my right hand grips her hair.

Her eyes look up at me innocently, but I know Saskia Hernandez is anything but. She's sucking my dick like she's a fucking pro. I know my girl will take my cock just as well.

I fight the urge to fuck her mouth, but she pushes my cock to the back of her throat as a go ahead, so I grip her curly locks tightly and thrust. Never letting my eyes falter, I tap the back of her throat repeatedly as mascara drips down her face. Her tits bounce each time I thrust further. She removes the hand from my cock for more length and grabs my ass cheek for stability. I grip her hair to hold it out of her face as sweat shimmers on her soft skin.

My body feels hot as my orgasm begins forming, my body suddenly feeling weightless. "Fuck, I'm going to cum." I growl, my jaw clenching as my dick hardens.

I can't control myself when she's what I'm looking at.

Hot, thick, ropes of cum eject from my cock as it lands on Saskia's tongue, like a fucking Picasso painting. I fight the stars in my vision so I can keep them on her perfect image but the ecstasy feeling engulfing my body is too compelling to fight. My muscles feel limp as I fight to stay still and I can't contain the moan that leaves my lips. My ears throb from my pumping blood, each beat from my heart echoes in my ear drum.

My hand wraps around Saskia's throat as I pull her to her feet, her tongue still painted with my cum. "Swallow." I instruct, my gaze meeting hers.

She does as she's told and swallows in one gulp before opening her mouth and showing me she obeyed. "Esa es mi chica buena." The words barely leave my lips before I'm crashing against hers, tasting my own release on her tongue.

Laying her on her stomach on top of the white blanket, she watches me in the mirror as I climb on top of her and open her legs. With a perfect view to watch me fuck her, I place gentle kisses down her spine as goosebumps assault her skin. Opening her legs slightly, I drop to my knees and line my cock up with her entrance, her pussy slick from her previous orgasm.

Slowly, I thrust all the way in, her mouth falling open as she adjusts to my size. I watch her palms grip the blanket as she arches her ass up, allowing me easier access. "Good girl." I praise. "Your pussy was made for me, Sas. You fit me perfectly." She nods between moans as I pick up my pace. My cock gets more slick as I fuck her, her body contouring to fit me perfectly.

I lean forward, my hands interlocking with hers as she looks in my eyes through the mirror. It's intense and erotic as our skin slaps together between thrusts. Fucking Saskia is a drug I'll never give up.

My mouth falls to her ear, my teeth nibbling on her soft skin as she whines, bucking her ass in the air. "Look at you taking me so well." I hum, my cock throbbing at the sight of Saskia watching her flustered self in the mirror. "That's my fucking girl." I pick up my pace as I kiss her soft shoulder.

Her whimpers become inaudible as she nods her approval, her hands clenching around mine. "Fuck, Mitch. I'm going to cum." Her voice is sulky as she sweat glistens on her bare back. Such a perfect fucking sight.

"Me too, baby. Fuck." I groan, my thrusts becoming erratic as I feel Saskia's pussy clench around my cock. Her pussy milks me as she screams her pleasure, arching her back further. Her grip on my hand is as warm as the hot cum spilling out my cock as my orgasm ripples through me. My sight is far from clear as white dots assault my vision and my ears thrum as my heart rate spikes. My weight feels invisible as my body gets lost in a world of bliss, unable to contain the grunts of satisfaction from leaving my lips.

I can barely catch my breath as we both finish, and as soon as I do, I look at Saskia and lose it again. She's a fucking goddess and and I want to be blessed to see her perfect self every single day.

Pulling out, I watch my cum ooze out of her entrance as I find some tissues to clean her up. She sits patiently as I finish, before I put her panties back on and zip her dress back up.

She uses some of the tissues to wipe the trails of mascara down her face and fiddles with her curls in the mirror as she pouts at her own reflection, before helping me get dressed. She buttons up my shirt, but freezes halfway up. I glance down, unsure what's wrong, but when I follow her eyes, I freeze up, too. I got a small red cherry tattoo on my arm for her, so I can always have her with me at all times. It was supposed to be a surprise for our anniversary a couple weeks ago, but I decided to save it for today, when I finally do what I've always wanted to.

She looks up at me with soft eyes, tears threatening to spill from her lash line, but I wipe them away before they can fall. "Turn around and stay there. Don't turn around until I say so." I tell her as sternly as I can as I rotate her body to face away from the mirror. I dart to the floral entrance and give a thumbs up to the two men in the vineyard, who return my thumbs up and begin running down with a wheelbarrow.

Saskia's getting impatient, but she doesn't disobey. It took a lot of planning and a few hundred dollar bills to make this work. Yet, her answer is the most important thing to me. The men set up the stand in front of the mirror, before running off with their wheelbarrow.

I take a deep breath and pull the ring from my back pocket. It's a gold band with red diamonds, a perfect match to her cherry necklace.

"Baby." I drop to one knee. "Turn around."

Saskia spins around, a smile on her face before she takes in the display in front of her. An edible cherry display that spells out *marry me* in front of the mirror, especially made for her enjoyment.

"Oh my god, Mitch." Tears begin falling as she steps forward, her hands over her heart.

"I can't imagine spending another day in this world where you aren't my wife. You bring such joy to my life and you made me realize that at thirty-five, I wasn't too old to be loved. You not only made me believe in love, but you gave me an opportunity to experience it with the most incredible woman." I grasp her palm as she beams down at me, sniffling between breaths. "Will you do me the honor of becoming my wife?" I ask, anticipation thick as seconds feel like minutes.

She nods frantically, wrapping her arms around my neck as I rise to my full height. Her legs are wrapped around my waist as she squeals, her excitement obvious in her grinning expression. As she drops to the floor, she holds her ring finger out and I slide the ring onto it.

Grasping my cheeks, she pulls my lips down to hers. "I fucking love you, Mitchell Alvarez." She coos, elation swimming in her irises.

"I fucking love you, too, cereza. Until the end of time."

I didn't realize I was in a dark place until I met Saskia. She threw down a rope and yanked me from the depths of my mind, into her world of color and enjoyment. She's my savior in the form of red cherries and gorgeous curls, which have turned out to be my two favorite things.

Since the second my eyes fell on Saskia in that courthouse, I'd dreamt she was mine. I've clung onto that feeling ever since, because it was unrealistic. Until it wasn't.

My cereza, my cherry, my Saskia.

*Mi amor.*

Like an eternal flame, my love has no limit and no ending for Saskia Hernandez.

## THE END

# *Acknowledgements*

Whew, where do I start? My soon to be husband, who pretends that the late nights writing don't bother him. Your constant support and encouragement is why you're my favourite person alive.

My friends, for their support and love. Especially you, Ellen! You are such a big reason I smash out books, because you are my biggest hype girl and I'd be lost without you!

My family, specifically my sister, who always reads my books, even though she can't focus on a task for longer than twenty minutes. Love ya, sissy.

My pup, who always keeps my toes warm when I'm writing by sitting on them. Mamma will always love your fluff on me.

My editor, Ria. You really put the work in on this one and made sure it all connected. I'd be lost without you. Thank you ten million times!

My BETA readers, Liv and Bree, who had amazing attention to detail and helped this story grow. I'll always value your opinions and I'm super grateful for your time and effort you put into this book.

My ARC readers, thank you so much for giving Restoring Justice a read. This small author is always grateful that someone wants to read my work, so thank you SO much!

And my readers, for keeping my books alive and keeping me going. I write for me, but also for you, so you can escape and read about the love you all deserve.

# About the author

Esme Lennon is an indie author from England. Her love for reading first started on Wattpad, where she read a few too many Marvel fanfics, and also began her writing journey. This led Esme onto booktok, immersing her in a world of contemporary romance and dark romance books. This gave her the courage and inspiration to write her own books and explore her own fictional worlds.

In her free time, Esme loves to lose herself in a good book and spend time with her fiancé, friends, family, and her pup. She's a complete home bird; you'll find Esme snuggled up on the sofa, re-watching Marvel movies with her better half.

# Also by Esme

Tainted Town Novella Series:
Little Snowflake – a stalker dark romance novella
Fractured Heart – a small town novella

Sin City Novella Series:
Power Play – a marriage of convenience novella